MURDER
on the
ROCKS

MURDER
on the
ROCKS

A Red Carpet Catering Mystery

Shawn Reilly Simmons

For Matt & Russell, My Rocks.

Chapter One

"Time to go." Sam Cavanaugh twisted the motorcycle's throttle as his girlfriend, Arlena Madison, swung her leather-clad leg over the seat behind him. "Hold on tight, bumpy roads ahead," he murmured smoothly as they pulled away from the curb.

Arlena looped her arms tightly around Sam's waist, her fitted jacket adorned with shiny silver zippers stretching across her back. She perched her chin on his shoulder after taking a quick look behind them.

They sped across the pitted asphalt, dodging an open-air sightseeing bus that trundled out from a side street. Several tourists wearing colorful ball caps swiveled their heads in Sam and Arlena's direction, then went back to studying Gothic architecture around them. Sam raised a hand in greeting, then flicked his eyes back and forth from the windscreen to the side mirror.

"Whoever is following us is getting closer, Jack," Arlena said after another quick glance to the rear.

"Not if I can help it," Sam said as he jostled the bike onto a stretch of cobblestones. The traffic light turned yellow, and he gunned it, blowing through the intersection.

"Hurry, Jack! They're getting closer," Arlena shouted, gripping Sam even tighter, strands of her long black hair whipping against her cheeks.

Sam steered the motorcycle hard to the right and cut down a narrow alley. Their follower did the same, turning at the last minute, skidding through a puddle and bouncing over the cobblestones. A blind man sitting in the alley raised a metal cup containing a few coins in the air as they passed.

Their pursuer was dressed head to toe in black leather with red slashes across the legs. A shiny helmet gleamed, a dark shield obscuring the face. Suddenly a gun appeared from the motorcyclist's tall leather boot. Swinging it up in a tightly gloved hand, a shot was fired at Sam and Arlena.

Arlena reached inside her jacket and pulled out a small silver pistol. She swiveled to return fire, her aim steady, her expression calm. The bike behind them swerved when Arlena pulled the trigger, her scarlet-painted lips pulling into a grimace. Arlena watched their hunter's gun bounce onto the cobblestones, and the bike decelerate and wobble as the driver struggled to regain control.

"Hang on!" Sam yelled. He took a quick left and nearly collided with a delivery truck parked in the adjoining alley. Arlena spun back around at the last minute, the gun jerking from her grip as they hit a pothole. It fell and bounced away from her, landing next to a stack of wooden crates filled with vegetables near the back door of a restaurant.

Arlena and Sam skittered onto a wider street, dodging through the narrow space between two slower-moving cars. Car horns blared loudly behind them.

"I think we're alone again," Arlena said. She twisted her head from side to side, looking over each shoulder. Sam made the next turn, then slowed his speed, relaxing a moment before his back tensed once again against Arlena's chest.

"No such luck," Sam said, nodding his head toward the whine of a motorcycle engine.

"Pull into the garage," Arlena suggested, pointing at a repair shop with an open bay door.

"We'll be trapped," Sam said grimly.

"Trust me, Jack," Arlena insisted. "You may be a master spy, but I know how to get out of a tight situation."

Sam eased the motorcycle into the garage, and Arlena's high-heeled boots stepped onto the oily concrete floor as he cut the engine. They stood shoulder to shoulder, their backs straight and their stance wide as they faced the open bay door.

The red and black motorcycle rolled into the garage and stopped a few feet away, the headlight cutting across the lapels of Sam's dinner jacket before cutting off abruptly. The same gloved fist that had pointed a gun at them moments before punched the button on the side of the bay door, causing it to rattle down to the floor. The garage grew dim as their pursuer reached up and removed their helmet. A wave of amber curls fanned across the woman's shoulders.

"Look what the cat dragged in," Arlena said with a sneering smile. She shifted her weight but kept her gaze steady. The woman shot Arlena an ugly glance, then held Sam's gaze.

"Cecily, imagine running into you here," Sam said, eyeing the dingy garage around them. "What are you doing in Prague?"

"I came to say goodbye," Cecily said icily. "We never got the chance in Paris. Imagine my surprise when I returned to our suite at *Le Meurice,* and you were gone."

"Ah, yes," Sam said jovially. "I'm afraid something urgent came up that I had to attend to right away."

Cecily eyed Arlena coldly, then slid her gaze back to Sam. "I see. Still, you could have told me, darling. I had to scramble to find someone to join me at the opera that evening. I was so looking forward to you being there."

Sam casually put his hands in his pants pockets. "I'm sure you were, my dear. Hopefully, the hitman you hired to kill me afterwards was able to make other plans as well."

"I don't know what you mean," Cecily said with a knowing smile. Arlena stayed silent as she eyed Cecily.

"Either way, the Paris job was done," Sam purred. "You gave me the codes. Your mistake was leaving your phone in the bedroom while you were in the shower." Sam shot an apologetic glance in Arlena's direction, which she ignored. "I saw the response come through, in code, of course, but I knew you'd hired someone to kill me. Another one of your mistakes. You should change your ciphers more often. You're a very chatty pillow talker. Word gets around."

Cecily's jaw hardened, and she bit her bottom lip. "I find it amusing you think you can simply use me and walk away. You've no idea who you're dealing with." Cecily pointed her chin at Sam. "I'm here to show you how wrong you are."

"Come on, Cecily," Sam said with a sly smile. "Some relationships aren't meant to last more than a few days. You would know that better than most. It was simply time to move on."

"Oh, I agree." Cecily removed a glove and unzipped her jacket, revealing a sleek tank top and ample cleavage. "I'm moving on as of this moment. I can't say the same for you two, though. Especially not when you're the only other person who knows the codes in and out of Plaza K. My superiors will know that information came from me." Cecily shot Arlena a condescending glance. "And I definitely can't let you get away with someone like her. You time has finally come, Jack Sloan." She slipped her hand to the small of her back, as if reaching for a weapon.

Arlena laughed sharply, the sound cutting through the stifling air of the garage. "What kind of woman chases after a man?" She darted her eyes at the windows behind Cecily, calculating how long it would take to reach the bay door. She took a few sideways steps away from Sam, who followed her lead and did the same.

"Stay where you are," Cecily said, revealing a small gun.

Arlena took another step, mirroring Sam's. "You can't shoot both of us," Arlena taunted.

"I can try. I'll start with you." Cecily took a menacing step forward, but Arlena held her ground. Sam eyed the closed garage door, listening to the traffic passing by on the other side. He swiveled his head slightly and took in the dingy paned glass windows on either wall, none of which were big enough for them to escape through. A small office was behind them on the left, but there appeared to be no other exits.

"Come on, Cecily. There's more than one fish in the sea," Arlena said, stalling. "Don't give up hope just because Jack isn't interested in you anymore."

Cecily tucked the gun back into her waistband and took a few steps closer, balling her hand into a fist and aiming it at Arlena's jaw. Arlena raised her forearm to block the blow, then grabbed Cecily's wrist and pushed it against her torso, shoving her away. Cecily stumbled backwards, then regained her footing.

"Don't worry," Cecily said, her eyes flashing. "He'll be through with you soon enough, too. Just like all the others before us." She picked up a length of chain from the floor and pulled it between her fists. "Get on your knees."

"No." Arlena reached down and slipped a folding knife from her boot, flipping it open to reveal a shiny silver blade.

"Careful, darling," Sam said evenly.

"Yes, careful darling," Cecily said sarcastically. She stepped closer to Arlena, the chain clinking in her hands.

Arlena set her jaw and raised her knife. "We'll be leaving now. Let's go, Jack."

Cecily scoffed and continued toward Arlena. "And watch Jack Sloan walk away from me twice in one week? I don't think so." She swung the chain suddenly at Arlena's head, who ducked out of the way at the last minute. Arlena reached out and grabbed the chain, pulling Cecily close. Arlena yanked the chain over Cecily's shoulders and spun her around, grabbing the gun from the small of her back and tossing it away. Sam darted toward the garage door, punching the button on the wall, causing it to roll upward.

Arlena wrapped the chain twice more around a struggling Cecily, who kept her eyes on the growing patch of light beneath the garage door and Jack Sloan smiling at her from the doorway.

Arlena spun Cecily back around, then leaned in, their noses almost touching. "Next time, you'll know when it's time to say goodbye." She pulled Cecily by her arm and shuffled her to the tiny office, shoving her inside and slamming the door. She picked up a nearby piece of plywood and wedged it under the knob.

Arlena strode across the floor to Sam and took his hand. He pulled her close, and they kissed in the open bay doorway, the radiant sunlight sparkling around them.

"We make a great team," Sam said, then kissed her again.

The image of the glamorous spies in love froze on the screen, and green script scrolled across: *Screen Test: Arlena Madison. Jack Sloan Film #5.*

Max Madison let out a low whistle and clapped three times. "Nice job, sis." He looped an arm behind her across the back of the white leather couch in Arlena's study. She smiled and elbowed her half-brother playfully in the ribs.

"That was so exciting," Penelope said. She sat in one of the soft leather club chairs in front of the fireplace. "The thought of you starring alongside Sam in the next Sloan movie! When will you know if you got the part?"

Arlena picked up a remote from the marble coffee table and turned off the television. "My agent says they're close to a decision. They're testing a few other leading ladies first," she said, a note of nervous apprehension in her voice.

"They're going to want you and Sam together in a movie again. Fans love that, an onscreen and off-screen romance," Max said confidently. "Hollywood gold. Think of the free publicity. People will be critiquing your chemistry, imagining your home life together."

"I know," Arlena said with less enthusiasm than Max. "We've been wanting to work together again ever since we met on *Remember the Fall*. And how cool would a follow-up like this be, going from an indie relationship film to a blockbuster action movie?"

"Why don't you sound more excited about it then?" Penelope asked. She got up from her chair and picked up their empty wine glasses from the marble coffee table, tucking them in the crook of her arm. Penelope was never completely out of her role as Arlena's personal chef, even though it was the weekend and Arlena insisted she take the day off.

"I don't know, Pen," Arlena said, chewing her lip. "Things are really good between me and Sam right now. What if the movie flops, and everyone blames me? Or even worse, what if working together in what's always been his domain messes things up for us?"

Penelope waved an empty wine glass in the air. "People love the Jack Sloan movies, Arlena. There's no way it's going to flop. And if, for some strange reason, it did, you and Sam have a stronger connection than that. I can't imagine you'd break up over a box office disappointment."

Arlena nodded, but a skeptical look remained on her face.

"The Sloan movies give the people what they love," Max added. "Master spy Jack Sloan meets a beautiful woman…or three…and an evil mastermind is outsmarted and ultimately thwarted after a half dozen car or boat chases. Then he rides off into the sunset with one of the helpful beauties after they save the world."

"Until the next movie," Arlena said. "Then there's a new beautiful super-spy."

"Yeah," Max said. "That's the drill."

"Didn't you say getting this part would be really great for your career?" Penelope asked.

Arlena sighed. "Yes." She stood up and hugged herself. "I'm overthinking it. If I get it, that's great. If I don't, that's fine too. It's all meant to be."

Max rolled his eyes at Penelope behind Arlena's back.

Penelope gave him a small shrug. "It's good you're preparing yourself for either option," she said encouragingly.

"Thanks. I'm starving. Let's order a pizza," Arlena said, abruptly changing the subject. "And watch a movie starring neither me nor my boyfriend."

"Or me," Max said, smiling. "Unless you want to watch the new episode of my show."

"Not tonight, Mr. Reality TV Star," Arlena teased. "I want to watch a film, not eavesdrop on the exploits of the young and famous of Lower Manhattan."

"Fine." Max tossed a throw pillow playfully at his older sister. "But no anchovies on the pizza this time, please."

Chapter Two

The next morning, Penelope and Arlena sat at an outdoor table at Sonya's Cafe, their favorite spot for brunch near the house they shared in Glendale, New Jersey. Penelope sipped a latte, and Arlena dunked an herbal teabag languidly in a mug of hot water as she gazed at the menu. Two men passed and did a double-take when they saw Arlena, a look of recognition on their faces. Arlena gave them a small smile, then tugged on the bill of her baseball cap and ducked her chin. She was becoming quite well-known as an actress in her own right, in addition to being the eldest daughter of acting legend Randall Madison and the girlfriend of action movie star Sam Cavanaugh.

"Glendale used to be such a sleepy suburb," Arlena said, glancing back at the menu. "Can you imagine I used to be bored here? Nowadays, it's like a mini big city."

Penelope glanced knowingly at the men, who continued to stare at the top of Arlena's cap as they passed by. Penelope edged her chair into the sunlight, out of the umbrella's shade, the sun's morning rays warming her shoulders.

Sonya, the owner of the cafe, appeared at their table wearing a pink t-shirt with the cafe's logo stretched over her broad chest. Despite the cool breeze, the hair at her temples was damp, and her brown cheeks glowed with red. "Lovely to see you this morning, girls. Sorry to keep you waiting."

"You're here by yourself?" Penelope asked, looking back toward the restaurant.

"My niece Mirabelle just showed up, thank goodness," Sonya said dramatically. "I was in the weeds, for sure, but I asked her to stop by the house and let Gigi out."

"Gigi?" Arlena asked.

"My little dog. She's old, can't hold it like she used to, and I've been in the kitchen since five this morning," Sonya said. "Anyway, what can I for you ladies?" She pulled an order pad from her black apron that had white flour hand prints over her hips. Penelope ordered Eggs Benedict, and Arlena chose the Lumberjack Special. "That's not your usual," Sonya chuckled as she scribbled, her thick forearms glistening in the sunlight. "You sure about that big breakfast, honey? Where you gonna put it all?" Sonya's Jersey accent rounded the edges of her words.

"I could eat this table right now," Arlena assured her.

"Okay, whatever you say," Sonya said with a chuckle before shuffling away.

"You've got a big appetite this morning," Penelope said. "Last night, too. I've never seen you eat three slices of pizza before."

"With anchovies. Max doesn't know what he's talking about. They're amazing." Arlena rubbed her palms together. "And now I'm craving bacon. Who knows what I'll be allowed to eat on our new set. Playing a professional athlete, I'm assuming I'll have to stick to some sort of regimen or another. I plan to enjoy my last few days of food freedom."

"I can always slip you contraband from the kitchen," Penelope said with a conspiring wink.

Arlena rolled her eyes. "I know you would, Pen," Arlena said. "My agent told me they hired a nutritionist for the set. A historian, too."

"A nutritionist? I suppose I'll be working with whoever that is."

Arlena craned her neck and looked toward the kitchen.

"The woman you're portraying played tennis professionally in the thirties and forties, right?"

"Yep. Helen Wills, the greatest tennis player of her time."

"What did women do to get in shape back then? They didn't have Pilates classes or gyms like we do now, did they?"

"I've seen pictures of Marilyn Monroe lifting weights. I'm sure Helen Wills had to be in top form to achieve what she did on the court." Arlena crossed her arms over her chest and squinted over the wrought iron fence that surrounded the patio. "Point is, whatever they say I need to do, I'm going to do. Biopics, when they're good, often get looked at come award season."

"Well, if they haven't had you dieting or pre-training before filming begins, I assume they think you're already pretty close to what they're looking for physically," Penelope said, tilting her face up to the sun.

Arlena's phone pinged inside her purse that was perched against the leg of her patio chair. While Arlena answered her text, Penelope watched a few people amble by on the sidewalk. Some held canvas bags of produce from the nearby farmers market, some jogged by with buds plugging their ears. Some were headed in the direction of the commuter train depot. Penelope breathed in the warming air, smelling the aroma of bacon mixed with the floral scents from the hanging baskets suspended on poles around the patio.

A ding from Penelope's own phone broke her reverie, and she sighed before reaching down to grab it. "Nadia will be here soon," Penelope said. "She asked me to order a black coffee and some yogurt with granola if they have it."

Arlena's nose crinkled with amusement. "I bet she'd like my breakfast better."

Penelope shrugged. "With the amount of calories I imagine she burns playing tennis, I'd think she'd just eat whatever she wanted."

"These are the kinds of things I'd love to hear more about so I can really get in the head of the character. I want to explore what it's like to push your body to its limits," Arlena said. "I hope Nadia can be friends with a bacon lover like me."

"I'm sure she'll like you," Penelope said. "You're both strong, successful women. You have lots in common when you think about it."

Arlena rubbed her chin with her finger. "Sometimes that can work against you with female friends. An opera can only house one diva."

Penelope watched out of the corner of her eye as Sonya's niece Mirabelle, a younger version of Sonya with long dark hair and bronzed skin, showed a couple with two small children to a nearby table on the patio. The little girl fussed at a ribbon holding one of her white-blonde pigtails until her mother gently pulled her hand away, distracting her with a stuffed giraffe from the diaper bag she slipped off her shoulder. The patio had been nearly empty when Penelope and Arlena had gotten to the cafe, just them and an old man drinking coffee in the back corner, but more people were entering the cafe and finding seats both inside and out.

"I think you and Nadia will get along fine," Penelope said, lacing her fingers together in her lap. "I've known her a long time. I wouldn't be friends with her if she wasn't a kind person at heart."

"When's the last time you saw her?" Arlena asked, sliding down her sunglasses to gaze at the young family, still maneuvering into their chairs.

"Only once or twice since high school," Penelope admitted. "We reconnected on Facebook several years ago. She's always posting beautiful pictures of herself during tournaments. Paris, London, beaches everywhere."

Sonya arrived with their breakfasts, setting their plates down on colorfully woven brocade place mats.

"Can I get anything else for you girls?" Sonya asked. She placed a hand lightly on Penelope's shoulder.

Penelope recited Nadia's order as Arlena dug into her breakfast. The little boy at the next table let out a loud cry, unhappy his father wouldn't let him pet the pigeon that had landed on the pavement near his chair.

"Get out of here," Sonya said, clapping sharply at the bird. It reluctantly fluttered away, landing on the opposite side of the fence. "Those pigeons are worse than rats. Scavengers," Sonya said as she headed back inside the restaurant.

"Penelope!" someone called from the sidewalk. She shielded her eyes and broke into a smile, waving at a tall woman jaywalking from across the avenue.

"Here comes Nadia now," Penelope said under her breath.

Nadia Westin was long and lean, and her strides covered twice as much ground as Penelope's. Her legs were wrapped in soft grey yoga pants, and a rose-colored t-shirt hung from her hangar-like shoulders. An orange leather bag dangled from her fingers, bouncing lightly against the side of her knee. Oval sunglasses obscured most of Nadia's face, but Penelope recognized her friend's strong jaw and toothy grin immediately.

"It is so great to see you again, Penelope," Nadia said, pausing on the other side of the railing.

"You too!" Penelope said. "Come on around."

Nadia looked for a gate on the fence, then followed Penelope's directions to go through the cafe's main door. A few moments later, she emerged onto the patio. Penelope stood up and gave her a hug, and Arlena stuck out her hand for her to shake. "Nadia Westin, nice to meet you," she said, shaking firmly with Arlena. The tendons on her tan wrist were as taut as piano wire.

"Thank you so much for coming," Arlena said as Nadia and Penelope settled into their seats. Arlena picked up her fork and pressed the side of it into the pile of pancakes on her plate.

"My pleasure," Nadia said. She adjusted her top and glanced around at the other diners as she placed her purse gently on the ground between her feet. Nadia slipped off her sunglasses to reveal almond-shaped eyes the color of roasted chestnuts. "I was so thrilled when Penny called. I'm a big fan of yours, Arlena. I've seen all of your movies."

"Oh wow, thanks," Arlena said after swallowing, blushing slightly. "And I've been watching you on the court the past couple of months. Quite impressive, especially this last Open."

Nadia nodded. "I don't know about you, but when I'm in the zone, playing tennis doesn't feel like a job at all. It's like I'm getting paid to do my favorite thing. Then I remember I'm at work when I'm getting ready for the season, all the training and mental preparation it takes. Sometimes, I want to just sleep in and eat a bag of chips for dinner."

Arlena chewed thoughtfully and waved her fork in the air. "Yes, I feel the same whenever I'm gearing up for a role. Like now." She took another bite of pancake and swallowed. "Sorry, they just brought out the food."

"Eat," Nadia said. Mirabelle dropped off a black coffee and Nadia's Greek yogurt and granola, gave them a quick once over then moved to the family's table to take their order.

"Penelope, say cheese." Nadia put one long arm around Penelope's shoulders and reached up her phone with her other, taking a picture of the two of them. She then pointed her phone at her breakfast and snapped a couple of pictures. Nadia slipped her phone back in her bag and took a sip of coffee. Penelope caught sight of a small stitched label under the top flap of her purse.

"That's a beautiful handbag," Penelope said, admiring the soft leather. A little silver lock dangled from the center.

"Thanks. My very own Birkin," Nadia said, rubbing the soft leather lovingly. "I had to wait months to get it. I treated myself after I won my first divisional."

"That's a good system," Penelope smiled. "Rewarding yourself for a job well done. You obviously have the discipline to wait."

"Well," Nadia said, "honestly, I had no choice. I was on a waiting list for it. You can't just buy one of them off the rack; you have to make it known you want one, then be patient." She brushed her fingers across the front of the bag, then sat up again.

Penelope took a closer look at Nadia's purse, resisting the urge to reach down and touch the leather.

"There aren't many movie stars from Glendale, New Jersey," Nadia said to Arlena, changing the subject.

Arlena shrugged. "Just me and my father, as far as I know."

Nadia nodded vigorously. "That's right! Randall Madison. I've seen him in a couple of things, but I was a fan of yours first. I looked him up because of you."

Arlena's shoulders straightened, and she set her fork down. "It's usually the other way around."

Nadia dipped her spoon into her yogurt. "So, tell me about the movie."

"It's a historical piece. I'll be playing Helen Wills, the famous tennis player."

Nadia placed the back of her index finger over her upper lip, her spoon dangling from her slender fingers. "The name rings a bell, but I can't quite remember."

"She was one of the first celebrity athletes," Arlena said, picking up her mug. "A trailblazer, really, for women in sports. She had lots of famous friends…actors, artists, politicians."

"Right," Nadia said. "It's beginning to ring a bell."

"So the movie, *Grand Slam*, is the story of her life, beginning with her dominant years in tennis. Helen was quite amazing. She was at the top of the tennis game for a record number of years in her day, but she was also an artist, a poet, and a writer. When she died at ninety-two, she bequeathed ten million dollars to Berkeley for neuroscience research."

"Wow, I had no idea," Nadia said. "I'm going to have to find out more about this woman."

Penelope took a bite of English muffin and watched a man stroll by, snatching glances at their table from behind his sunglasses. He had close-cropped blond hair and a long beard, popular with the hipster crowd, more and more of whom had been moving into Glendale in greater numbers. A small smile played on his mouth, and Penelope caught sight of a purple stain on his lip. It was a little early in the day to be drinking red wine, she thought. Maybe he'd just had a blueberry smoothie. Penelope tried to picture Joey, her clean-cut boyfriend, with a hipster beard and laughed to herself.

"It's great this movie is being made, that there's broad interest in a female athlete," Nadia said. She set her spoon down and leaned forward. "Who will be playing Helen in her later years? I assume it will be you for the rise to fame period, when she was young and beautiful, in her prime."

"I'm playing her at all ages," Arlena said.

"What? That's amazing." Nadia's mouth hung open for a second as she studied Arlena's face. "How is that possible?"

"Makeup, wigs, prosthetics," Penelope said. "It will be a total transformation. It's my first time attempting a broad character age range on a movie."

Nadia kept her gaze on Arlena, eyeing her youthful skin and slender neck. "That's something I'm really looking forward to seeing."

Arlena laughed. "Me too. I assume they'll do work in post-production, use computer effects to smooth things over, make sure I look realistic."

"That is something else," Nadia said. "So you want to know what it's like to be a tennis pro, and that's where I come in."

"Exactly," Arlena said.

"Well, I can tell you all about my own experiences, but I'm not sure I can help with what Helen's life was like. I'm not close to having ten million dollars to donate anywhere," Nadia said, pulling her lip down in a half frown.

Arlena laughed. "I've been researching Helen's life, and there's going to be a historical consultant on set who will answer any time-period-related questions. What I was hoping you could help with would be the physical part, the ins and outs of tennis, the mindset of an athlete, especially one who plays a singular sport as opposed to on a team. I'd love for you to provide any insight you can so I'm the most convincing. I'm really interested in any challenges you may have faced, how the victories feel. With your help, I think I can nail this."

Nadia turned and put a hand on Penelope's shoulder. "This is so exciting," she whispered.

"I know," Penelope said. "I'm glad you're available to do it."

"It's good timing, my season is over," Nadia said. "I have a few months off before I have to be back on the circuit."

A pair of teenage boys walked by on the sidewalk, hockey sticks strapped to their backpacks, heading toward the community park. Penelope's eyes moved over them as they walked quickly by, their forward-leaning postures, their matching haircuts, one dark and one reddish-blond. Then her gaze came to rest on the bearded hipster she had noticed before. He was across the street, leaning against a lamppost near the bus stop, staring down at his phone. He looked up suddenly, but his sunglasses prevented Penelope from seeing if he was looking at their table or just in their general direction.

"One of the important events the movie will dramatize is the Battle of the Sexes tournament where Helen beat Phil Neer, the eighth-ranked male tennis player at the time," Arlena said, digging back into her breakfast.

"Wasn't that between Billie Jean King and Bobby Riggs?" Penelope asked, pulling her attention back to the conversation.

"That one happened years later. The very first one was at Wimbledon in 1888," Arlena said. "Helen was the third, and she was the first female to win one."

"Someone has been doing background research," Penelope said.

"That must have been something to see," Nadia said. "I wonder how Helen's opponent took the defeat."

"According to what I read in the script, not great," Arlena said with a sly smile.

"I can imagine. Especially back then. It's still hard for the guys to lose to one of us," Nadia said.

"So that's it," Arlena asked. "And working with Penelope and the nutritionist for my meal plan. You'll be paid per diem as a consultant. And you'll get a film credit. I've already confirmed that with the director."

Nadia sat back in her chair and put a hand on her chest, a grin spreading across her face. She reached down and pulled her phone from her bag and said, "Can I get a photo of us so I can remember the moment I became a movie consultant?"

Arlena hesitated for a second and then said, "Sure." Nadia popped up from her chair, and she and Arlena smiled at the device while Nadia snapped several photos.

"I'll tag you," Nadia said, retaking her seat.

"Oh, I'm not on social media," Arlena said. She watched Nadia type quickly with her thumbs.

"What?" Nadia asked. "Not even Facebook?"

Arlena smiled sheepishly. "Nope."

"Your publicist doesn't think you should have an online presence?" Nadia asked distractedly.

"I don't have a personal publicist," Arlena said, shrugging at Penelope.

"Each movie has a promotional team. I haven't seen the need to hire one of my own."

Nadia set the phone down. "Interesting," she said under her breath.

Penelope listened to the conversation, but kept the man across the street in her peripheral vision. Arlena had been approached many times by over-enthusiastic fans, both on movie sets and in regular life. Penelope had gotten used to being more vigilant when they were out together, for Arlena's safety as well as her own.

"Anyway, use me however you want. Maybe I can give you some social media tips too—" Nadia was cut off by a happy squeal from the next table. The little girl with the ribbons in her hair was clapping at the Mickey Mouse pancakes Sonya had placed in front of her.

Nadia smiled at the family. "I wonder what it's like to have children so close together in age, all babies at the same time."

Mirabelle approached their table with a coffee pot held tightly in her fist. "Refill?" She reached over to begin pouring before Penelope could answer. "Anything else we can do for you ladies?"

"As a matter of fact," Nadia began, picking up a nearby menu and looking through it quickly. "Do you have fresh avocado?"

Mirabelle pointed at the menu with her pinkie. "Yes, it's there under the sides."

"Are they ripe, though?" Nadia asked. "I can't stand under-ripe avocados. I like them on the soft side."

The girl nodded crisply, her ponytail bouncing on her shoulder. "I'm sure they are, but I can check before bringing you some."

"Great, I'll do that then. And an order of turkey bacon—"

A crash sounded behind them when a pitcher of ice water smashed onto the ground from the corner of the patio. One of the boys Penelope had seen earlier on the sidewalk had placed his backpack over the sharp points of the railing and jumped onto the patio. He pulled the bag back over his shoulders and began shouting at the stunned diners, who either stared at him, mouths open, or stood up quickly from their chairs. He yelled what sounded like "plate it" several times, his face red and shiny from sweat, his dark hair stuck to his forehead. He waved his hockey stick in an arc over his head, then crashed it down onto the table nearest him, sending plates and glasses flying. Someone inside the restaurant screamed, and a car horn sounded on the street.

The young man then flipped the table over, and the couple sitting at the next closest one scrambled away, toppling their chairs as they ran inside the restaurant. Penelope stared at the boy for a second, frozen to the spot, in disbelief that this was happening. The straps of his bag pulled down his shoulders, and Penelope irrationally wondered what was inside the dark blue satchel. The word bomb crossed her mind and spurred her into action.

"Get down!" Penelope shouted to Arlena as she jumped up from her seat and moved toward the family with the children. Arlena was frozen, staring at the far end of the patio before reacting. Mirabelle bolted towards the restaurant with Nadia close on her heels, her purse clenched tightly to her side. "Let's get out of here!" she shouted back over her shoulder to Penelope.

The mother leapt up and pulled the little girl from her booster seat. The child wailed in protest, her cheeks turning an angry pink.

Penelope reached her hands out to the woman. "I can take her. Get over the fence and I'll hand her to you."

The woman stared at Penelope in shock, then hugged the toddler closer to her chest. She turned away and stared at her husband. He had followed her lead and grabbed their son, who was letting out his own squeals of protest.

Penelope heard another crash and watched the young man swing at one of the flower pots suspended over the patio with his hockey stick. The clay burst into pieces, and soil and flowers flew through the air before falling to the ground.

"Go over the railing," Penelope urged the couple, who watched several people retreat into the dark interior of the restaurant.

The woman looked back at her with a terrified expression, then at the spikes on top of the wrought-iron fence. She finally nodded tightly and turned back to her husband.

"Follow me," he said to his wife and started toward the restaurant door. The woman threw Penelope a glance of startled apology, then followed him. Her husband crushed their son to his chest and hurried inside, the little boy's feet dangling at his belt.

Penelope ducked under the table where Arlena was hiding and grabbed her wrist. "Let's get out of here." She flicked her eyes at the fence.

"Wait, no!" Penelope heard someone shout and then another crash and a cry of pain. She peeked out from under the table and saw the boy swing his stick in an arc, then head inside the cafe. The older man who had been sitting alone on the patio was holding a hand to his forehead, blood streaming through his fingers.

Penelope's knees weakened. "Someone's hurt," she said, working to keep the alarm out of her voice. Arlena's arms grew rigid as she pulled them around her torso in a hug. "Call the police," Penelope said, eyeing Arlena's bag on the ground. "I'll go help him."

Arlena's hand clasped Penelope's wrist and pulled her back just as she began to stand up from her crouching position. "No," Arlena said simply. "What if he comes back out? What if he has a gun?"

"A gun?" Penelope asked.

"How can we be sure he doesn't have a gun?" Arlena said firmly. She released her grip on Penelope's wrist and dug in her purse for her phone.

Penelope watched the dazed man as he sat on the patio and listened to Arlena whisper to the emergency operator, trying to decide how injured he was. A flash of red near the front door of the cafe caught

Penelope's attention. She straightened her back and eased forward slightly, craning her neck to get a better view. Their attacker's companion, the one she'd seen him with earlier on the sidewalk, was leaning casually against the front door. Penelope watched him eye an older couple walking by, his reddish blonde bangs flopping over his forehead, and reach slowly into a side pocket of his cargo shorts. Penelope's heart began to race when she thought about a gun being hidden there. The couple veered off just before they reached the cafe and jaywalked across the avenue, a large dog on a leash pulling him toward the park, the woman talking on a phone pressed tightly to her ear. Penelope looked toward the now-empty bus stop and the passing cars on the street. No one driving past seemed to notice anything out of the ordinary happening at Sonya's.

Penelope heard yells from inside the restaurant and the words "plate it" again. She thought the boy had some kind of accent, but the sounds from inside were muffled, and she couldn't place it. The boy guarding the front entrance looked up and down the sidewalk after the door bumped him from behind, then pressed his back harder against the wood.

"What is he doing in there?" Arlena hissed in a panicked whisper after she hung up with 911.

"Not sure," Penelope said. "A robbery, maybe?"

"In broad daylight?" Arlena asked.

Penelope shrugged. Another crash from inside convinced Penelope to act.

"What about Nadia?" Arlena asked, darting glances toward the restaurant.

"His partner is guarding the door. She's trapped in there with everyone else."

"We have to get out of here," Arlena urged.

"Yeah," Penelope said, looking up at the fence behind them. "The spires on top look sharp, but maybe we can use a chair."

"It's to keep the pigeons off," Arlena said. "I'd rather get poked by a fence than attacked by a violent maniac with a big stick."

As they inched closer to the railing, Penelope looked back at the man on the patio. He'd begun to crawl their way, his progress slow.

"We're not leaving him behind," Penelope said. A sickening series of thuds and a hoarse scream from inside the restaurant made Penelope's legs go weak.

Arlena edged a chair closer to the fence, making a loud scraping sound on the cement. Penelope's heart rate quickened when she thought about them attracting attention to themselves out on the patio. She took a deep breath and hurried to the man. She crouched down next to him and gently pulled his arm over her shoulders. "Let's go," she said as she helped him up and moved quickly back to where Arlena was waiting. Penelope grabbed a napkin from one of the tables and handed it to the man, who held it against his bleeding head.

The sound of a siren approaching provided temporary relief, quickly replaced by panic when she thought about how the boys might react when they learned the police had arrived.

Arlena helped Penelope onto the chair and waved for her to go over first. "We'll help him from both sides," she said in an even voice. The man looked at Arlena doubtfully as Penelope made her way over. The old man clambered onto the chair, then toppled awkwardly over the fence, falling onto Penelope, who did her best to keep them both on their feet. Holding onto the railing, she managed to steady herself, then helped Arlena meet them on the other side of the fence.

Penelope felt a sense of lightness and intense relief as they stood on the pavement. She peered around to the front door of the restaurant and saw the accomplice who had been holding the door closed was gone. People from inside the restaurant were tumbling out the door, and a few people had gathered on the sidewalk, watching them emerge.

Some were squinting curiously at the panicked faces of the diners. One man held his phone aloft, recording the scene. Penelope's knees began to shake as a burst of adrenaline rushed through her.

"We're safe now. It's going to be okay," Arlena said.

"What about Nadia and that young family?" Penelope asked, her voice much louder than she'd intended it to be. "He's still in there with them."

Arlena hugged Penelope close and eyed the man they'd helped over the fence. He was perched on a ledge of the building next door, muttering to himself, the white napkin turning red from his blood.

A police car screeched to the curb, and two uniformed officers jumped out. They scanned the gathering crowd before rushing toward the front door of the restaurant. Several people stepped forward to try and speak with them, but they waved them off as they drew their guns and hurried inside. A second patrol car arrived shortly afterwards, and those officers began ushering the onlookers to the opposite side of the street.

"Did you get a good look at him?" Arlena asked.

"No," Penelope admitted. "It's weird because someone just before caught my attention, and I was kind of focusing on him. It seemed like he was looking at us too closely or something. But maybe he wasn't watching us at all. Maybe he was just a guy at a bus stop." Penelope laughed suddenly, then placed a hand over her mouth.

"Penelope, what are you talking about?" Arlena asked gently. "Are you okay?"

Penelope dropped her hand from her mouth and nodded. "Sorry. I didn't get a good look at the boy inside, but I did see the one guarding the door. I saw both of them, kind of, I guess."

"Well, at least you saw something," Arlena said. "I was taken totally off guard. I was so focused on talking about the movie with Nadia."

Just then, a gunshot rang out from inside the restaurant. The small crowd that had gathered on the sidewalk ducked down as a group, a few of them backing further away from Sonya's.

"Oh no," Arlena said.

The old man looked at them with a stunned expression from behind his napkin. "The children," he muttered.

An ambulance bounced up the avenue, coming to a stop at the curb, sirens off.

The mother of the two small children emerged from the front door of the restaurant, escorted by one of the officers. She held a crying toddler in each arm, keeping them pressed against her torso, her expression a mask of terror.

"Where's their dad?" Penelope asked, taking a step closer.

A faint radio crackle drifted across the air, and the paramedics sprung into action, hurrying into the restaurant.

"If they're letting the EMTs in, they must have gotten that maniac under control," Arlena said.

One by one, people exited the cafe, most visibly shaken, some crying and looking around like their surroundings were unfamiliar. A few pressed cloth napkins to their faces. Penelope couldn't tell if they were to wipe away tears or to tend to injuries. A bulky man in a stained white apron had a bloody towel wrapped around his forearm. An EMT guided him toward the ambulance.

"Sir, we should get you some help," Penelope said to the man with them. "What's your name?"

"Fred Eames. And I'll be fine," he said. He pulled the napkin away from his forehead, and Penelope saw a purplish welt and a gash. The bleeding appeared to have slowed, she noticed gratefully.

"Mr. Eames, you've got a head wound..." Penelope said.

"Worse things have happened to me," Mr. Eames said. "Let them look after the women and children first." Penelope looked down at his shiny windbreaker and a collection of small pins. They looked military in nature, with emblems, stars, and stripes, one in the shape of an eagle.

A paramedic emerged from the cafe and called to the ambulance driver. "I need a hand." He nodded and joined her, then the two of them wheeled a stretcher into the restaurant, the wheels bouncing over the cracks in the sidewalk.

"Who would do something like this?" Mr. Eames said, shaking his head. Arlena sat down next to the man on the ledge, and they both stared toward the cafe.

Another ambulance pulled up just as the first set of EMTs rolled a stretcher carefully through the front door. Penelope caught her breath. "Look!" She took a few stiff-legged steps toward the cafe, keeping her eyes on the young father's face, which was red and pinched with pain. His left arm was secured in a stabilizing cast. Penelope was relieved to see Nadia behind him. Her jaw was set in a defiant line, and she appeared to be uninjured.

The last people out were Sonya and her niece, Mirabelle. Their arms were linked tightly together, and they leaned into each other as they stepped gingerly to where the ambulances were waiting. Sonya's cheeks were wet with tears, but looked to be unhurt.

Mr. Eames sighed loudly, and he attempted to stand up from the ledge, but his legs wouldn't hold him. Arlena urged him to stay put, and he reluctantly nodded and sank back down. He kept his eyes trained on the people emerging from the cafe.

"Nadia!" Penelope called as she approached the fence. Nadia scanned the crowd outside until her eyes landed on her old friend.

"Nadia, are you okay?" Penelope asked, thinking that, of course, she wasn't. But what else was there to say?

"I'm fine," she said quickly, a hand wrapped around her wrist.

"What happened in there?" Penelope asked gently.

"It was awful," Nadia said, shaking her head. "All of those innocent people, suddenly under attack. We were trapped. Scared."

Penelope looked down at Nadia's wrist, which was beginning to swell.

"Let's get someone to look at that," Penelope said. The EMTs were rushing around, helping people who were bleeding or in obvious distress. The chaos was unnerving.

"We heard a gunshot. Did he have a weapon besides his hockey stick?"

"Not that I saw."

"If they captured him, where is he? They haven't brought him out yet."

Nadia shook her head. "From what I overheard, he must have escaped out the kitchen door through the back alley."

"What?" Penelope asked. A shot of fear coursed through her. "How can that be?"

Nadia pressed a shaky hand to her forehead. "He broke that man's arm, the one with the kids, because he got in front of his family after he took a swipe at me." She looked down at her wrist and her voice broke. "Then that maniac dragged that poor young father into the kitchen when he heard the sirens approaching. His eyes were wild, like he was out of his mind. Pure hatred." Her eyes flicked to the ambulance that was just pulling away from the curb. "Then the police came in, and we pointed to the kitchen. Next thing we heard was a gunshot, the door slamming, and then silence, which was scarier than anything else."

Penelope's feeling of relief was replaced with anxiety and an overwhelming sense of being exposed. "So they're both still out there."

"Both?" Nadia said, looking confused. Penelope told her about the boy she'd seen guarding the front door.

"They're gone," Nadia mumbled the last words more to herself than anyone else.

"They can't be," Penelope said, startled by the feeling of tears welling up. She fought them back and watched a police officer study Sonya's front door from the sidewalk. "I'm going to go tell him about the other boy," Penelope said. "Make sure they know to look for two of them."

Nadia just stared ahead. She lifted her wrist higher in the air and continued to massage it.

Chapter Three

"There were two," Penelope said. "They worked together."

The officer nodded as she spoke, his hands on his utility belt. They stood on the sidewalk outside the cafe, a few steps away from where the ambulances were idling.

"So you got a good look at the suspects?" he asked.

"Yes, I think so," Penelope said. She focused on what she remembered about the boys, holding on to pieces of detail in her mind before they faded, the similarities and differences in their features. "And I don't suspect anything. I know what they did. I saw them walking by on the sidewalk a few minutes before the attack."

"Most likely casing the place, making their final plans before they made their move," the officer said, looking at her curiously.

Penelope watched another officer open the cafe door and prop it with the rubber kickstand on the base. "There might be fingerprints on the door."

The officer gave her a small smile. "Of course, we'll check for them. We'll dust the whole place, matter of fact."

Penelope ignored his slightly sarcastic response and let her gaze wander to the enclosed patio and the debris left behind, a colorful sea of overturned tables, menus, purses, place mats and napkins, phones, and smashed tableware. Her eyes fell on a dark blue backpack lying on its side under one of the tables. "He had a backpack on, too. I thought it was weird he kept it on, then I wondered if it was part of the plan."

"Plan?" the officer asked.

"I don't know, maybe he had weapons in there, or a bomb."

The word bomb caused the officer's expression to darken. "Or it was to collect the spoils of the robbery," he said. He walked away from her and began talking on his radio, alerting the other members of the team to be on the lookout for a dark-colored backpack.

Penelope saw Nadia leaning against the remaining ambulance, pressing an ice pack to her wrist and staring at the patio. She walked over and put a hand on her friend's shoulder. "Does it hurt badly?"

"No, I've been injured worse than this before. The man who stepped between me and that kid is the one who got hurt badly. He took all the blows to protect us." Nadia's eyes were glassy and held a faraway look.

"I hope his injuries aren't too severe," Penelope said.

Nadia stiffened and shifted away from her touch, still staring at the cafe. Penelope pulled her hand away.

"When are they going to let us back in to get our things?" Nadia asked. "My bag…my phone, my keys, everything is still in there. They wouldn't let us bring anything out with us."

Penelope watched an officer place yellow numbered markers on the ground amid the broken glass and other items strewn across the patio. "They're processing the scene now. They're not going to want it disturbed until they document exactly what happened."

"But why my things? I'm one of the victims," Nadia said with a tinge of impatience.

"You know, they just can't. It's procedure."

"Yeah, I've seen all the television shows," Nadia said with a sigh.

Arlena approached them, supporting Mr. Eames as they made their way slowly over, her arm entwined with his. She got the attention of one of the paramedics and waved her over, pointing at the welt on Mr. Eames' head.

"He's still saying he doesn't want any help," Arlena said. "But it's better to have someone look at it, right?" He shook his head carefully but followed her lead.

"Especially with a head injury," Penelope said. She spotted Sonya speaking with one of the officers. "I'll be right back."

When Sonya saw Penelope approaching her hands went to her cheeks. She hurried over and pulled Penelope into an embrace, her strong arms wrapping shakily around Penelope's ribs.

"I'm so sorry," Sonya said. "Thank goodness you're safe."

"Don't be sorry," Penelope said. "We're fine. I just wanted to make sure you're okay."

"Ma'am?" the officer said, bringing her attention back to him. "You were saying?"

"Right," Sonya said, releasing Penelope. "Like I said, I never saw those boys before, no time, never once in my place."

The officer scribbled something on a notepad. A dark blue unmarked police car pulled up to the curb nearby, and Penelope's chest warmed. Her boyfriend, Detective Joseph Baglioni, stepped out of the car and onto the pavement. His eyes fell immediately on Penelope. She hurried to him, and they met halfway on the sidewalk, stopping just short of an embrace.

"You hurt?" he asked. His expression was concerned, his jaw clenched.

Penelope shook her head. Tears pricked her eyes, and her throat closed up.

Joey's face softened, and he pulled her into a hug, kissing the top of her head quickly. Penelope pressed herself against his broad chest and closed her eyes, wishing the feeling of his arms around her could last forever. But it was just a quick squeeze before he pulled away. His expression hardened when he saw the cafe's patio.

A woman in jeans and a brown leather blazer stepped from the passenger side of Joey's car. "I'm heading inside," she said as she stepped onto the curb next to them.

"I'll be in shortly, after I get a briefing." The woman nodded at him sharply, her eyes skimming across Penelope's face as she passed.

"Who's that?" Penelope asked. She watched the woman take long strides toward the front door, running her fingers through her cropped red hair before stepping inside.

"Detective Clarissa Hightower, my new partner," Joey said flatly. "Just temporary, from what I hear. She's mid-transfer, on her way to a sergeant's desk in Newark. Something about us being shorthanded and needing a department restructure. They've parked her at our station for a while until they fill a few more seats."

Penelope couldn't tell if the sharpness of his tone was due to his being annoyed by having a new partner, or if he was just worried about what happened at Sonya's. Or both. He took Penelope gently by the arm and guided her to where Arlena and Nadia stood together on the sidewalk. A few feet away, Mr. Eames sat on the bumper of the ambulance, a paramedic shining a light in his eyes and asking him questions. Penelope watched him look behind her to where Sonya spoke to the officer on the sidewalk in front of her cafe.

"How are you doing?" Joey asked Arlena.

Arlena shrugged. "We're lucky the police showed up when they did, and the kid didn't have time to come after the rest of us out on the patio. Mr. Eames here was the first one attacked. He was sitting in the corner where the kid came over the fence." She nodded toward her new friend, who was speaking in an even voice with the EMT.

"That's my table," Mr. Eames said, interrupting the paramedic. "I always sit there."

"Lieutenant Eames?" Joey asked, taking a few steps toward the ambulance.

"Retired," Mr. Eames said. "Ten years now."

"Detective Baglioni," Joey said. The EMT looked over her shoulder back at Joey, who motioned for her to continue her treatment of the retired officer. She pressed a white cloth to Mr. Eames' forehead, causing him to wince. "Can you tell me what happened?"

"Like the actress said," Mr. Eames said, waving at Arlena. "Punk popped over the fence and knocked me one on the noggin. And down I went. I don't know any more than that."

Joey sighed. "Okay if I ask you a few more questions when they're done fixing you up?"

"You can ask," Mr. Eames said grumpily. "But I don't know anything else."

The EMT placed a white bandage over the cut on his head, and Mr. Eames closed his eyes, dismissing Joey and any further questions. Joey turned back and introduced himself to Nadia, who shook his hand limply and remained silent.

"I'm surprised they don't have a way to enter and exit the patio," Joey said, eyeing the pointed iron fence.

"It's probably that way to keep their things safe," Penelope said. "Not having easy access keeps people off the patio when the restaurant is closed. They don't have to lock up their tables and chairs every night."

"The people who were inside look like they've been through hell." Arlena paused. "Sorry, Nadia," she added.

Nadia cleared her throat. "It's okay." She cradled her wrist in the crook of her other arm, balancing the cold pack on top of it.

"If robbery was the motive," Penelope said, "there are certainly easier targets than this one." She thought about the pharmacy on the next block, the bodega, and the little coffee shop. They would all have been easier to get in and out of and would have had fewer people inside to deal with. "What would make Sonya's a target for them?"

"Lots of people with cash and wallets," Joey said. "And the register, of course."

"And run the risk of being trapped and almost shot?" Penelope asked doubtfully. "Feels like pickpocketing people on the street would be less dangerous."

"Whatever they were trying to do, they're not going to get away with it," Joey said. "So maybe they knew all along they were going to hit this cafe."

"They got the money from the till, and then they started grabbing wallets," Nadia said after clearing her throat.

"That's what the backpack was for," Penelope said. "I had a crazy thought that he had weapons or something else more dangerous in there."

"He may have. I didn't really see inside," Nadia said.

"They were prepared," Joey said. "And they came for a fight."

"With big sticks," Penelope said.

"And those who didn't want to turn over their things, he'd just start hitting," Nadia said matter-of-factly. She pressed a hand to her mouth as if she was feeling sick.

"Did either of them say anything you can remember?" Joey asked.

"The one with the stick kept saying 'plate it'. I didn't hear him say anything else," Penelope said.

"He was saying the word 'pay' over and over," Nadia said quietly. "In Russian, *platit* means pay."

Arlena looked at her doubtfully. "Are you sure? I couldn't tell what he was saying, to be honest. He just sounded crazy."

"I heard what he said," Nadia said, her eyes flashing. "I heard him."

"Right, he was asking for your wallets," Joey said, sighing.

"Did he seem to be asking anyone in particular?" Penelope asked.

Nadia shook her head. "He was taunting us, the owner, the cook from the kitchen. He sneered at us, threatened us."

"He didn't mention anyone by name, by any chance, did he?" Penelope asked.

"Not that I remember," Nadia admitted.

"Okay. You've all been through a lot today. Why don't you head home, and I'll check in with you in a little while," Joey said.

A crowd had gathered on the opposite sidewalk, and Penelope could see a couple of phones pointed at them, recording their exchange.

Arlena smiled at Joey gratefully. "I don't want my being here to draw any unwanted attention to Sonya and her family." She flicked her eyes at the crowd on the sidewalk, then tilted her chin away and pulled on the bill of her baseball hat.

Joey nodded. "You guys drive or walk here?"

"We walked down, and Nadia took the train over from the city," Penelope said.

Nadia turned her back to them and fixed her gaze on the cafe. "When can we get our things back?"

Penelope could make out hers and Arlena's purses on the patio, along with a few other bags, phones, sunglasses, and other personal items strewn across the ground among the tipped-over tables and chairs and the smashed flower pot.

"After the team inside is finished, we should be able to release your items back to you," Joey said.

"But my wallet, my keys," Nadia protested. "How am I supposed to go anywhere without them?"

"You can stay with us as long as you need to," Arlena said. "We're just a few blocks away. I trust the police will get our things back to us quickly."

Nadia seemed about to protest, but, after a few seconds gave in with a weak shrug. "I guess that's my only choice at the moment. The paramedic said I should go get an x-ray. I told him I didn't think it was broken or anything." She held her wrist limply in her hand.

"I'll drive you to the hospital," Penelope said.

"I don't even think I have to go," Nadia said, sighing. "I've jammed it worse in the past on the court."

"You've got the movie coming up and lots of training in the next couple of months with Arlena. Maybe it's better to be safe than sorry," Penelope urged. She watched the paramedic guide Mr. Eames into the back of the ambulance. "You want to ride with them, and I'll meet you there?"

"Sure, if they have room," Nadia said. She went over and spoke to the EMT as she jumped down from the back. Penelope saw her nod and guide Nadia inside the ambulance, then close the doors.

"I'll be in touch soon," Joey said. He gave Penelope a quick kiss on the forehead and nodded at Arlena, then headed for the front door of the cafe.

Chapter Four

Penelope surveyed the waiting room at Glendale's Medical Center. Rows of faded blue bucket seats were harnessed together, anchored by tables on each end, with only a few empty seats available. A large flat-screen television was bolted to the wall opposite the intake area, where two receptionists greeted incoming patients. Penelope walked to the edge of the room and leaned against the wall.

She gazed at the TV and watched a smiling woman with long red hair on a set designed to look like a home kitchen, slicing squash and sliding it into a simmering pot, making frequent eye contact with the camera. A caption below her announced she was preparing her version of Ratatouille with fall vegetables. Penelope watched with interest, silently critiquing the chef's knife skills while she waited for news about Nadia.

A woman stood up on the far end of the room, her back to Penelope. When she turned her head, Penelope recognized her as the mother of the small children from Sonya's. She stepped gingerly down the aisle and headed toward the restroom on the opposite wall from the one Penelope leaned against. After she pushed through the door, Penelope thought for a minute, then crossed the room and followed her inside.

Penelope washed her hands in the sink and gazed at her reflection, noticing her eyes were a bit puffy. The young mother came out of one of the stalls and sidled up to the sink next to Penelope's, flicking her a quick glance in the mirror. A glimmer of recognition flitted across her face, but she stayed silent.

"How are you doing?" Penelope asked.

The woman's expression shifted in the span of a few seconds from fearful to angry. "As well as you can expect," she said quickly, then her features softened. "I appreciate you trying to help us back there. We should have followed you out instead of going inside. Were you hurt?" She looked at Penelope's arms and hands in the mirror, as if looking for injuries.

"I wasn't hurt. I'm waiting for my friend," Penelope said. She turned off the water and pulled a paper towel from the dispenser on the wall. She handed it to the woman and tore one for herself. "How are your children?" Penelope asked gently.

The woman sighed and wiped her hands. "They're okay. Luckily, my parents live close by, so they took them home. My husband has a concussion; his forearm is fractured. They want to monitor him here overnight." The woman vibrated with a nervous energy.

"I'm sorry to hear that," Penelope said. "I'm glad he didn't hurt the children. I'm Penelope, by the way. I live over on the north side."

"Kelly Leterneau." The woman pressed the paper towel to her lips and blotted them a few times. "I think he would have if he'd gotten the chance. He didn't have any regard for us, even the children," she said darkly. "I looked in his eyes. I didn't see anything there, no compassion."

Penelope crossed her arms loosely over her chest and leaned against the wall. "Do you remember him saying anything? Like why he was in that particular place?"

Kelly thought for a moment, then threw her paper towel in the trash bin behind them. "It was all gibberish, what I heard."

"I heard he spoke Russian, maybe," Penelope said.

"I guess. I don't know it, but it sounded something like that," Kelly said. "He did seem to want money. Especially valuable items like our purses. I just don't understand the brutality. We would have given up our things."

Penelope thought about Nadia and her expensive bag. Maybe not everyone.

"Did it seem like he'd been in the cafe before? Like he knew Sonya?" Penelope asked. "I still don't understand why her place became their target."

"Maybe," Kelly said. "I don't know. When he hit that woman on the arm, we knew we had to hand over our things. He went right for her, no hesitation. The sound of that stick against bone was sickening." Kelly reached out and steadied herself against the sink.

"The tall, dark-haired woman?" Penelope asked.

"Yeah," Kelly said. "After he attacked her, that's when my husband stepped in. Got in between that monster and the rest of us."

"He's very brave. Please tell him we're grateful he did that," Penelope said. "The woman he attacked, she's my friend."

Kelly nodded like it was understood. "I have to check on him, then get home to the kids. The doctor ordered more scans, but they should be done by now. I want to say goodbye before I go."

"Of course," Penelope said. "Good luck to you all."

Penelope watched her push through the bathroom door and leaned against the cool tiles on the wall. She thought about what it had been like inside the cafe, the pain inflicted, the fear everyone had gone through. The heroes inside and outside who had banded together to help. She cleared her throat and then went back out to the waiting room.

"I'm sorry, I can't give you any more information." One of the receptionists was speaking to a man in the window, her voice louder than Penelope had noticed earlier.

"Tell me where she is," the man demanded. Penelope approached from behind, recognizing the windbreaker from earlier in the day.

"Mr. Eames?" Penelope asked.

"It's lieutenant," he said sharply.

"How are you feeling?" Penelope said, glancing at the receptionist, whose expression was one of closed-off annoyance.

"Wha-, oh, yeah," Mr. Eames put a hand to the bandage on his head. "Just a scratch. Punk kid didn't realize how hard my head is, I guess." He turned his attention back to the woman sitting in the chair behind the window. "Tell me how she's doing."

"I'm sorry, sir," the woman said flatly. "Again, if you're not family, I can't share information about another patient."

"I've known Sonya for more than thirty years," Mr. Eames huffed. "That should count for something."

Penelope eyed the receptionist, who had turned her attention to her monitor. "Do you have a ride home?" she asked Mr. Eames.

Mr. Eames sighed but didn't answer. He shuffled past Penelope and out the front doors of the medical center into the bright sun of the afternoon.

Chapter Five

"Thanks for picking me up," Nadia said as she and Penelope entered through the back door and into the kitchen.

"Of course," Penelope said. "I'm glad the doctor confirmed nothing was broken." She looked around the familiar room, her safe place, grateful to be home. A sudden weariness overcame her, and she pulled out one of the stools from the counter.

A barrage of high-pitched barking from Arlena's side of the house and the scraping of tiny toenails on the floor got louder as Zazoo, Arlena's Bich-poo, scurried into the kitchen. His fluffy white hair bounced comically on his small head, and he seemed to smile up at Nadia while tap dancing with excitement.

Arlena came into the kitchen and scooped him up, snuggling him to her cheek. "Hush," she scolded playfully. "We have company," she said before setting him back down on the slate tiles. He scurried to his little red bed in the corner and plucked a rawhide chew stick from his pile of toys.

"Let's have some wine," Arlena said with a sigh. She moved to the cabinet without waiting to see if she had any takers.

"Can you make mine a vodka gimlet?" Nadia asked. "If you have any vodka on hand."

Arlena paused while reaching for the wine glasses. "Sure," she said. "Why not? A change of pace for us, right Pen?" She reached below the counter and pulled out a bottle and a cocktail shaker.

"Limes are in the fridge," Penelope said, standing up to help.

"Sit," Arlena insisted. "I got it. You want one too?"

"Absolutely," Penelope said. "Sounds perfect."

"I love wine, but this kind of day calls for a real drink," Nadia said. "Hope I'm not being too forward."

"Nadia, please," Arlena said, eyeing the sleek silver shaker. "After what you've been through today, ask for whatever you please. Plus, you're our guest."

Nadia smiled gratefully. Penelope propped her chin on her palm. She watched Arlena add ice to the shaker, and mix together vodka and lime juice, then expertly pour the same amount into the glasses.

"I didn't know you were such an accomplished mixologist," Penelope said with admiration.

"I had practice growing up, mixing cocktails for my mom. Manhattans, mostly. And many years later, I played a bartender in a TV pilot that never got picked up. *Bottoms Up*. Kind of glad that one didn't see the light of day. But it was a good drink-making refresher course."

"Here's to method acting, immersing yourself in a role," Penelope said, raising her glass before taking a sip.

Nadia took a large drag on her cocktail and set the heavy crystal glass back on the counter.

"Did the doctor prescribe any pain meds?" Penelope asked.

"Yeah, but I don't need them," Nadia said. "I'm used to physical pain, unfortunately. And pain meds mess with my stomach. I'll stick to gimlets."

"What happened was awful, and I'm sorry you got hurt," Arlena said, becoming serious. She took a large sip. "But we can still have a positive start to our friendship. I know we're going to have a really good experience on set."

Penelope gazed at her glass and swirled the pale green liquid.

"Pen?" Arlena said. "You okay?"

Penelope shook her head and smiled weakly. "Yes, I'll be fine. It's just the shock of it, I think. The idea that something so random can happen to anyone, something so life-changing, just when you least expect it."

"Exactly. Unfortunately, things like that are happening every day, all over the world," Nadia said, nodding in agreement. "It's hard to wrap your mind around."

Arlena peered inside the shaker, then mixed another batch of drinks. Penelope felt the edges softening, her taut muscles relaxing, a serene feeling washing over her. Arlena filled their glasses a second time.

"Let's do something for Sonya," Arlena said. "She's a long-time member of our community who could use our support. What do you think, Pen?"

Penelope brightened a bit. "That's a nice idea. It's a small business, they probably have insurance, but the rates go up if someone is injured. And if Sonya has to cover herself and her employee's wages…what happened could end up costing her a lot of money."

"Okay," Arlena said with determination. "I'll approach Sonya and see where we might be able to help. We can't change what happened, but maybe we can help make it a little less traumatic."

Penelope's eyes drooped, and she yawned. "Guys, I think I have to lie down for a while. I'm feeling totally wiped out." She took the last sip from her glass and set it down carefully before sliding off of the stool.

"Me too," Nadia said. "Adrenaline crashes are the worst. I get them all the time after a big match."

"I'm sure we could all use a nap," Arlena agreed.

Penelope yawned again and waved a sleepy goodbye before heading upstairs to her room. She pulled back her comforter and slipped into bed, falling asleep to the murmured conversation in the kitchen below.

Chapter Six

The sound of a car making its way up the driveway woke Penelope. Her mouth tasted bitter, and her head was heavy from a sound sleep. The light filtering through the gauzy yellow curtains was warm and fading, and she realized she'd napped away most of the afternoon.

Penelope got up and gazed out over the front lawn and driveway. She was happily surprised to see Joey's car pulling around the side of the house. Her mind slipped back to the events at Sonya's, and a feeling of uneasiness gripped her. Images of their attacker and the calm look on the face of the other boy holding the door closed, trapping the helpless people inside, made her shudder.

Penelope pulled the band that dangled from the end of her disheveled ponytail. She ran her fingers through her long blonde hair, scraping her short nails against her scalp to shake away her thoughts. She flipped on the light in the adjoining bathroom and rolled her eyes when she saw the red creases from her comforter pressed into her cheek and pools of mascara smudged beneath her eyes. She quickly brushed her teeth and splashed warm water on her face before heading downstairs to greet Joey.

Penelope slipped down the smooth wooden stairs in her bare feet and headed to the kitchen, where she heard the familiar voices of Joy, Arlena, and Nadia, and a woman she didn't recognize saying hellos and making introductions.

"Penelope, look who's here," Arlena said. She'd changed into a pair of jeans and a tight t-shirt, a small strip of tan flat stomach showing just above her waistline. Nadia was perched on the edge of a stool at the counter, rhythmically tapping the countertop with the fingertips of her uninjured arm. Penelope saw she'd removed the bandage on her wrist. The skin was bruised, but the swelling had gone down.

"Hi," Penelope said, her voice still thick with sleep. Out of habit, she hugged Joey tight. He gave her a small squeeze in return.

"Penny," Joey said, "this is Clarissa Hightower." He nodded at his new partner, who was half a foot shorter than Joey, but still taller than Penelope.

"Nice to meet you," Penelope said, sticking out her hand. "I saw you earlier at the…at Sonya's," Penelope stammered, then cleared her throat.

Clarissa nodded and shook her hand firmly, then tucked her fingers into the pocket of her jeans. "I'm sorry we didn't meet under more pleasant circumstances."

"How is the investigation going? Have you tracked down those boys yet?" Penelope asked. She waved at the stools tucked under the island's counter as an invitation to sit, but Clarissa shook her head.

"I'm afraid we have bad news," Joey said, then hesitated.

Penelope recognized the expression of dread on his face, and she braced herself for his next words.

"The owner of the cafe, Sonya Harper, has passed away."

The room fell silent for a moment, then Arlena said, "No, that can't be right. She wasn't injured in the attack. We saw her afterwards, walking out unharmed. She was with her niece Mirabelle."

Clarissa and Joey exchanged a glance.

"That's right," Penelope said. "It was the cook who was injured, but he's not the owner. His head was bleeding. Not Sonya's."

"Yes," Clarissa said, "one of the cooks, also a family member of Sonya's was assaulted by our suspect when he tried to intervene during the altercation. Mirabelle was also assaulted during the incident."

"Assaulted?" Arlena asked.

"Yes, her forearms sustained some bruising from where our suspect grabbed her when he threw her against the wall. Apparently, she'd gotten between him and Sonya during the attack."

"Wait, none of what you're saying explains how Sonya died," Arlena said. "What happened? Did she get assaulted by the kid, too?"

"No," Joey said. "Sonya and Mirabelle went to the hospital together and were released. When they got home, Sonya began experiencing chest pains and collapsed. The paramedics were called, but by the time they arrived, it was too late. She died of a heart attack at home."

Penelope once again felt the unpleasant closing of her throat, her breath constricting.

"And you still have no idea who they are or why they did this," Arlena said angrily.

"It was a robbery," Nadia said. "Greed, pure and simple."

Joey sighed and dropped his eyes to the floor. "We're still looking for specific answers. One theory is they hopped a train down at the station and headed out of Glendale. There were three departures shortly after the police arrived on the scene."

Penelope sat down heavily on one of the stools. "You're assuming they left together. If it were me, I'd split up from my accomplice. And maybe I wouldn't take the next train, maybe I'd find a place to hide out downtown until the police activity died down, slip away later."

"True," Joey said. "Those are all good points."

"And," Penelope said, tapping a finger on her bottom lip, "what if they had disguises in their backpacks, hats, different shirts, something to change into that would throw you off their scent?"

Clarissa folded her arms at her chest and listened to Penelope with interest. "We've thought about that too," she said evenly.

"Are there cameras at the station?" Arlena asked.

Joey nodded. "We're reviewing the footage now."

"But if they've managed to disguise themselves, what good are they?" Arlena asked, deflating a bit.

"We don't know that they have," Joey said. "If they thought ahead and planned their attack to coincide with the train departures, Sonya might not have been a random target. At least it shows some thought was put into the plan."

"We realize this is difficult," Clarissa said with a twinge of exasperation. "Members of your community were involved in a brutal attack. We'd like to go over the events again to see if there's anything else you might remember that could help us find these guys."

"I honestly think I've told you everything I remember," Penelope said.

"Sometimes things surface later," Clarissa said. "You may remember something out of the blue in a few days that could be helpful."

"What about cameras on the street?" Penelope said. "There were people on the sidewalk. Someone must have filmed what happened on their phone."

Clarissa nodded. "We've put out an alert asking for people to come forward with information, contacted the local news outlets. Did you recognize anyone at the scene, a neighbor or acquaintance that we can contact?"

Penelope thought about the man at the bus stop, then shook her head. "No one I know personally."

Nadia tapped her foot lightly on the floor.

"We've collected security footage from a nearby bank, but it doesn't appear any cameras were pointed directly at the cafe," Clarissa said. "Sonya's doesn't have an advanced security system, just a simple alarm at the front and back doors, nothing fancy. Our techs are searching for the suspects by filing through whatever sidewalk footage we've been able to obtain."

Penelope thought about downtown Glendale, its quaint old architecture and historic buildings. She knew there weren't many cameras, and until now, she didn't think there was a need for them. "So, if they didn't walk by and look directly into the bank camera…"

"Or the train stations…exactly," Clarissa said. "Plus, with the farmers market in full swing on one side of town and people heading to the park on the other, that's a lot of faces to look through."

"They should be able to pick out two boys carrying hockey sticks pretty quickly. Maybe they knew how to avoid being caught on tape," Arlena said.

"The one stick was left at the scene in the kitchen," Joey said. "We haven't located the second one, but it will probably end up in a dumpster somewhere. Penny, did either of them have any distinguishing features? Scars, a tattoo, a limp, anything like that?"

Penelope thought for a moment, picturing their faces, the one on the patio's expression of twisted rage as he yelled at the patrons. A finger of fear slid down her spine. She took a deep breath and said, "I'm sorry, no."

"It's okay, Penny," Joey said. His expression was hopeful but contained. "Nadia, you mentioned the one inside was speaking Russian. How can you be sure?"

Nadia dropped her hands onto the counter and gazed at him with watery eyes. "I trained in Kazan when I was first starting my career. I've gone on tours, played all over Russia."

"Have there been any other robberies like this one in Glendale?" Penelope asked. "I can't remember any."

"Robbery might not have been the real motive," Clarissa said.

"What do you mean?" Penelope asked.

Clarissa shared a glance with Joey, who shook his head slightly.

"The suspect ditched his backpack in an alley near the cafe. We recovered all the wallets and the cash from the till."

"That's great," Penelope said, relieved.

"Why would he ditch it?" Arlena said.

Joey shrugged. "He got scared, thought if he didn't have the stolen money with him, he'd look less guilty if caught. Who knows?"

"Sonya died for no reason at all," Penelope said softly.

Clarissa cleared her throat, then rested her gaze on Nadia. "We've been able to account for all the personal items, confirm they belong to the cafe's customers. The only thing missing is your bag."

"What?" Nadia asked sharply, sitting up in her chair. "No, that can't be right. It was inside on the bar with all the other purses. I saw it there when we were led out. The officer wouldn't let me grab my things before we were shuffled out the door."

"Unfortunately, she's correct," Joey said. "We've been able to identify all the other personal belongings through identifications inside or descriptions from the victims."

Nadia stood up from her stool. "Someone took it? You need to find my purse," Nadia raised her voice, causing Zazoo to stop chewing his rawhide stick and prick up his ears at her.

"It may have been misplaced," Joey said. "Our people are going through the evidence boxes as we speak. We'll find it, I'm sure."

"And if you don't?" Nadia asked sharply.

"We'll take a report from you and send it through the proper channels. If it has been lost—"

"Or stolen," Nadia interjected harshly.

"Or stolen," Joey continued carefully, "we'll take the necessary measures to compensate you for your lost items."

Nadia laughed sharply. "Wonderful news. I hope they're ready to hand over ten thousand dollars, because that's what I paid for my Birkin after waiting on the list for half a year to get it."

Everyone in the room stared at her in stunned silence.

"We're looking into it," Clarissa said. "Procedure will be followed. If there's been any impropriety, we'll file charges against those responsible."

Nadia balled her hands into fists and glared at them. Penelope saw her wince slightly at the tenderness in her wrist.

"I have both Arlena's and your things in the car," Joey said quietly to Penelope. "I figured I'd bring them over and save you a trip to the station." Clarissa glanced at him, and her jaw tightened. He ignored her.

"Thanks, Joey," Arlena said. "That was thoughtful of you. Nadia, I'm so sorry this is happening, but I trust Joey as much as anyone I know. He'll find your bag."

Nadia turned away from them and stalked out of the room toward the library.

Clarissa followed Nadia's progress out the door as she spoke. "We'll need her to come to the station and file a report on the missing bag. We'd also like you to sit with a sketch artist, Penelope, describe the suspects so that we can get a usable image of their faces to distribute."

"Okay, I can do that," Penelope said.

"We should get back," Clarissa said. "If anything else comes to mind, we'd appreciate a call. We'll see you at the station in the morning."

Chapter Seven

"This day went from terrible to downright awful," Arlena said after Joey and Clarissa had stepped out of the kitchen door to get Penelope's and Arlena's things from the car.

"Nadia seems really upset about her purse," Arlena said in a low voice. "I mean, I can see why."

"It's worth ten thousand dollars?" Penelope said in a stunned whisper.

Arlena nodded knowingly. "That's on the low end, if you want to know the truth," she whispered, glancing toward the hallway leading to the library. "They're one of a kind, hand-made by one person. It's a total status bag."

"Do you have one?" Penelope murmured, pantomiming a purse over her shoulder.

Arlena shook her head. "No. I'm not sure I want one. I've read some things about how the animals are treated, and it sort of put me off. Plus, I can think of a lot of things to spend that kind of cash on before an accessory."

A flash of motion caught Penelope's eye through the window of the back door. Penelope saw Joey and Clarissa out on the patio, standing next to a table. Joey had his hands on his belt and was leaning toward Clarissa. She had her arms crossed tightly, and her head tilted slightly to the side while she listened to him.

Penelope kept her voice low as she watched them through the glass pane on the window. "I'm sorry about Nadia's bag, but Sonya's dead. And poor Mirabelle, what that girl has gone through today…it's hard to imagine what she's going through."

"It's a tragedy," Arlena agreed. "What are you looking at?"

"Nothing," Penelope said, continuing to stare.

Joey shook his head at something Clarissa said, then turned and stalked away from her, heading around to the driveway. Clarissa watched him for a moment, then followed.

"I'm going to see if Joey needs help," Penelope said, slipping off of the stool. She stepped into a pair of garden clogs she kept on the bottom shelf of Arlena's antique wooden coat stand next to the door and went outside.

The air had cooled as the sun dipped almost out of sight. The scent of lilacs drifted over from the flower patch Arlena had asked the gardener to put in earlier in the summer. Fall hadn't technically arrived, but it would be there in a couple of weeks. The evenings were growing shorter with each passing day.

Penelope followed the slate path around to the garage and paused near the edge of the concrete driveway. Joey was speaking in a firm tone, tinged with irritation.

"There's nothing that says I can't bring a witness their personal belongings myself, especially one who was directly affected by the events of the crime. Also, you could have told me before we drove out here you wanted Penny to come in and sit with the sketch guy," Joey insisted. Penelope heard the trunk of his car groan open. She stayed just out of sight and listened.

"Of course, I want an admitted eyewitness to sit for a drawing, and you should, too. Standard procedure is to have them come to the station and sign for their things," Clarissa said evenly. "You want to do personal favors for your girlfriend, that's fine. But don't make it seem like that's what's always done."

"It's not a personal favor. It's a courtesy to a traumatized witness," Joey said.

Clarissa scoffed. "Call it what you want. I don't see you driving any other purses around town."

Penelope peeked around the corner of the garage and watched Joey rifle through the trunk. His jaw was tight, and his expression dark. He pulled the trunk closed, hers and Arlena's purses clutched in one of his large hands. "You didn't have to come with me, you know."

"We're partners," Clarissa insisted. "I'm just pointing out this trip wasn't necessary. The real reason we're here is so you can do favors for your friends."

"Look," Joey said, his face reddening. "We're working together now. For how long, who knows? Let's try and get along. You can start by not selling out our department, assuming we have a thief at the station."

"I don't need to get along with anyone to do my job," Clarissa said. "And neither do you. That's what regulations are for."

"That's a great way to look at things," Joey said sarcastically.

"Look, we're going to work together fine as long as you don't expect me to go outside the rules."

Joey shook his head and started walking toward where Penelope was hiding. She turned and hurried to the back door, where she kicked off one of her clogs. She reached down and pulled it back on, adjusting the strap across her heel just as Joey turned the corner, acting as if she'd just stepped outside.

The look of irritation on his face remained, but it softened when he saw her. He looked back over his shoulder and, seeing Clarissa hadn't followed, set the purses down on the patio table and went to Penelope. He put one hand on her neck and pulled her in for a kiss, slipping his other arm around her waist and holding her tightly against his body.

Penelope kissed him back, her heart hammering in her chest. Joey nuzzled her neck and whispered in her ear. "I'm so glad you're okay. I love you."

"I love you too," Penelope whispered back. She rubbed her cheek against his stubbly chin.

"You're everything to me," Joey said. "The thought of you getting hurt, or worse. I just can't—"

"Shh," Penelope said, kissing him softly on the lips.

"When are you leaving again?" Joey asked in a husky voice.

"Day after tomorrow," Penelope murmured. She pulled away from him and looked into his dark brown eyes. "We're staying and working out of the director's house on a lake near Micklesburg, Vermont."

"You know I'm going to miss you like crazy," Joey said. "With us not having a full team at work for this case, it might be difficult for me to get away to visit this time."

"I understand," Penelope said. "Let's play it by ear. I won't be as far away this time; it's just a few hours' drive North."

"Come and stay with me tomorrow night," Joey said. "I have to work during the day, but I want to spend some time with you before you leave."

"I'd love that," Penelope said. She perched her chin on his shoulder and closed her eyes, breathing in the fading scent of his soap.

The sound of Clarissa clearing her throat behind them caused Joey's arms to tense at her waist. He reluctantly pulled away. "Okay then," he said, clearing his throat. "I'll just bring your things inside, get your signatures, and then we have to get back to the station."

"Okay," Penelope said, wobbling slightly on her clogs.

Joey grabbed the bags and headed inside. Penelope followed him, glancing back at Clarissa as she reached the door, whose lips were pressed together tightly as she glanced around the patio and the adjoining gardens.

"Can I get you anything before you go? A bottle of water, some coffee?" Penelope asked.

"No thanks," Clarissa said with a tight smile.

55

Chapter Eight

The next morning, Penelope rose early and headed out for a run at sunrise. She went over the conversation that she'd heard between Joey and Clarissa the previous evening once again. It had kept sleep just out of reach for over an hour as she lay awake in bed. Despite her nap, she'd been exhausted, but her mind wouldn't settle long enough for her to doze off. She didn't want to cause Joey any trouble at work, or be looked on like she was getting special favors from him. She also didn't know how or if she should bring it up to him.

Her thoughts turned again to Clarissa. Going by first impressions, she appeared strong and confident. Joey hadn't had a dedicated partner before, at least not since Penelope and he had been dating, going on two years now. Penelope smiled when she remembered seeing Joey for the first time again, right there in her own kitchen. He'd been the lead detective then too, when she and Arlena had discovered a dead girl near their property. Joey had changed quite a bit from their middle school days together. Now things were getting serious between them, and Penelope thought how lucky she was, having come across her old friend again and their friendship having grown into much more.

Joey had always worked on his own, it seemed to Penelope, only occasionally asking for backup support from the other detectives in his station. Glendale was a small town without much crime, but it was still a suburb of New York. Penelope supposed some coarser elements from the city could very easily leak their way into town, especially with the train station right there.

Penelope had purposely left her phone at home, not wanting anything to get in the way of a peaceful morning run, even her music or the encouraging mechanical voice of the woman on the running app she used.

Penelope increased her pace and ran down a side street, away from her usual route. She'd decided to go for a longer run that morning since the following day, she'd be traveling with her catering crew and back to work on a brand-new movie set. Her personal time was always limited when she was working, so she'd learned to enjoy it when she could. Once they got to Vermont, they'd have to shop for food, order supplies, plan the first couple of weeks of menus for the cast and crew, and lay out their kitchen and workspaces.

Penelope's breath was even, and she fell into her comfortable faster pace, listening to the neighborhood around her waking up as the faint hum of traffic rose from the highway in the distance.

She took another turn onto Glendale's main street and slowed to a walk, squinting a few blocks down the avenue at Sonya's cafe. Yellow police tape fluttered in the morning breeze, but otherwise, things appeared as they always did this time of day. The streets were quiet, the morning rush of commuters not yet up to full force.

Penelope entered the coffee shop on the corner. "Good morning, Lois," she said as she approached the counter. "Can I get a black coffee to go?"

"Sure thing, Penelope. You're up early again today," Lois said.

"Yeah," Penelope said, biting her lip. "Crazy thing yesterday over at Sonya's." She looked down at the newspaper rack at the *Glendale Gazette*'s headline: **Sonya's on Main Street Scene of Brutal Attack**. She scanned the first two paragraphs of the article. Her eyes fell on a photograph of Sonya, smiling in a checkered apron and holding a full plate of eggs, bacon, and toast.

"You have to ask yourself, what kind of a person does something like that? And with the children there." Lois's statement died away as she poured Penelope's coffee and set it on the counter.

"Did you happen to see the boys they're looking for yesterday? You have a view of the cafe from here, right?"

Lois placed a palm on her wrinkled cheek and shook her head. "I've been trying to think on that, and I wish I had. I saw all the commotion afterwards, of course, but nothing out of the ordinary beforehand. I told the officer who came by yesterday. Some neighborhood watch captain I am, right?"

Penelope smiled and pulled two folded dollars from the interior pocket of her running shorts. "Sorry they're a little damp."

Lois waved her off. "It's on the house, Penelope."

"You sure?" Penelope said, holding out the money.

"I heard you were there helping yesterday," Lois said. "We need more people like you, less like them."

"Them?" Penelope asked.

"You know, criminals who go after innocent people and their families while they're enjoying breakfast together," Lois said.

Penelope tucked the bills back in her pocket. "I didn't do much, really. Just climbed over the fence."

"Stop it. You were very brave," Lois said. "I heard about how you tried to help some of the people over. I only wish they had listened to you instead of going inside with him."

The blush on Penelope's cheeks deepened. "Well, you never know what you're going to do in a situation like that. I'm glad it wasn't worse than it was."

"Me too," Lois said with a slight frown.

Penelope shook her head and glanced back down at the article. She scanned it quickly and didn't see hers or Arlena's name mentioned, which she was grateful for.

"Okay, dear, do me a favor and watch out for the crazy drivers while you're out running. Kids today with their texting, and iPads, distracted all the time. More respect should be paid to your neighbors, you know what I mean?"

Penelope took a small sip of coffee to hide her smile as she pictured someone driving with an iPad in their hand. Although she was sure it had happened somewhere. "Yeah, I know what you mean, Lois. Thanks again for the coffee."

Penelope stepped back outside and walked quickly down the side-walk, holding her cup a little bit away so she wouldn't spill any on herself. She slowed as she passed Sonya's, taking a good look at the patio. The tables and chairs that had been toppled over the day before had been set back on their feet, but were scattered haphazardly across the clay tiles, not in the usual neat rows Sonya preferred.

A flash of movement behind the windows caught Penelope's attention, and she squinted through the tinted glass, resting her hand lightly on the metal gate that she and the others had climbed over the day before. A shadow shifted inside, and Penelope saw a man move through the dining room and into the kitchen, carrying something large in his arms. A strip of reflective material ran across the shoulders of his windbreaker. Penelope saw the letters P and O before he turned, and assumed it was someone from Joey's team, gathering more evidence inside.

Penelope sipped her coffee and took a few steps to where she and Arlena had escaped. A metallic taste filled her mouth, and she looked away quickly and tossed her half-empty coffee cup into a nearby trash can on the sidewalk. She reached out to hold onto the gate, a fingertip brushing a torn-off piece of yellow police tape.

In the distance, the train horn blared. She crossed the street, slowing her pace as she neared the bench at the bus stop. A couple of commuters waited nearby to catch the first bus into the city, a man in a suit staring at his phone and a younger woman in a transit uniform holding a thermal mug of coffee. Penelope stepped behind the bench and grabbed the post under the bus stop sign, pretending to stretch her calf while she looked across at the cafe. She pictured herself and her friends at the table the morning before and thought about the man who seemed to be watching them from this spot right before the attack began.

Penelope noticed the bus schedule encased in scratched plastic on the pole. Running her finger down and over, she noted the times listed. A bus was scheduled to stop a few minutes before the time of the attack.

A large orange and white bus with the letters NJ in a circle roared up to the stop, and the commuters rose from the bench and climbed aboard. Penelope watched them each flash a pass at the driver.

"Coming aboard, ma'am?" the driver shouted through the door when he saw Penelope lingering by the bench.

"No," Penelope said, shaking her head. The driver started to close the door. "Wait!" she called to him. The driver paused and reopened the doors.

"Come on up," he said in a hurried tone, flashing a glance at the watch on his wrist.

Penelope climbed up the first step. "I just wanted to ask, were you driving yesterday?"

The bus driver gave her a smile, his teeth a light shade of yellow. "Sure," he said. "Who wants to know?"

"Did you hear about what happened over there?" Penelope flicked her eyes across the street at Sonya's cafe, then to his uniform shirt, where a small silver nameplate read KING.

The bus driver rubbed his chin and nodded. "Yeah, I did. Saw some commotion across the way, too. When I read about what happened in the paper, I couldn't believe it."

"Did you see what was happening, Mr. King? That there was a violent attack underway?"

The old man shook his head, his expression hardening. "No way. I would have called it in to HQ if I'd seen anything like that. I report stuff all the time, suspicious folks all over the roads around here. I called in a drunk driver last week, in the morning!" Mr. King wheezed a raspy chuckle, then coughed into a handkerchief from his pocket.

A man in the front row cleared his throat loudly and rustled his newspaper. Mr. King looked in the mirror attached to the windshield, then at his watch again. His hand slid to the lever to pull the door closed. "Have to get going now. Schedule to keep."

"Wait, do you remember a man getting on the bus around one yesterday afternoon? He had a beard, blonde hair, I think. There was a dark stain on his lip."

The bus driver chuckled and shook his head. "Let me think. Nope, I don't remember anyone like that. I don't spend a lot of time studying faces, though. Just the road and the clock."

Penelope sighed and went to step off the bus. She turned back quickly just as the driver pulled the doors almost closed. "How about a younger man, actually a teenager with a hockey stick? Dark hair? He slipped away during the attack."

The driver nodded. "I may not remember faces; you know I see hundreds of those a day. But I always notice a potential weapon. Part of my training is to be prepared for anything, keep the passengers safe. I've seen hockey sticks before. And Baseball bats, packages left behind, duffel bags clanking on the floor that made me uneasy. I've seen everything on this bus line the last ten years."

"What about yesterday? Did you see anyone with a hockey stick yesterday?" Penelope urged.

"Come on, let's go, driver," a passenger called from behind Mr. King.

"I may have, I'd have to think. Maybe not. One day is a lot like the next behind the wheel." He brushed his fingers on the bill of his cap and smiled at Penelope again before closing the doors on her. The bus lurched down the avenue toward the New York skyline in the distance. As the bus pulled away, Penelope held her breath to avoid taking in the exhaust fumes.

A fresh scratch in the paint on the bench caught Penelope's eye, and she got closer to get a better look. Running her finger over it, she felt the smooth edges of the groove, then turned and headed to the train station.

Chapter Nine

A couple of hours later, Penelope and Nadia drove to the police station together to file the report about Nadia's missing bag. "Are you okay?" Penelope asked. Nadia had been mostly silent during the short trip to the station.

"It's hard not having any of my things. I don't even have the keys to my apartment," Nadia sighed.

"I know," Penelope said. "Hopefully, everything will be found soon."

"Not if the police took it," Nadia said with a sarcastic laugh.

"What do you mean?"

"The guy ran out of the restaurant with the police on his tail. He didn't have my bag with him," Nadia said. "It disappeared afterwards." She inserted air quotes with her fingers, "in police custody."

"Come on, let's get inside," Penelope said. "I'm sure Joey will figure this out."

Penelope watched Nadia and Joey talk through the glass of one of the small conference rooms lining the main floor at the police station. Joey filled in a form as Nadia spoke, offering her encouraging smiles in between questions.

"Excuse me, are you Penelope Sutherland?" A short man with graying hair and a mustache asked as he approached the seating area.

"Yes," Penelope said, standing up.

"I'm the sketch artist. They've asked me to sit with you this morning?"

Penelope followed the man into a small office on the opposite wall, and they sat next to each other, facing a computer screen.

"Are you ready to begin?" the man asked. He wore a tweed vest over a gingham shirt and a bright red bow tie. The smell of stale coffee permeated the air around him, and a slight whiff of tobacco.

"We have numerous descriptions of suspect number one," he paused and picked up a folder, flipping through several pieces of paper with yellowing fingers. He handed Penelope a printout of a composite sketch of the boy who attacked them. It was a good likeness of the teenager, Penelope thought, as she studied the fuzzy ink lines that made up the face.

Penelope took a deep breath. "From what I remember of him, this is pretty accurate."

"Good," he said. "Our focus today is suspect number two, the one..." he consulted a report from the folder, "...who you claimed was the lookout at the front door. We don't have a description from any other witness on him yet."

Penelope set the composite sketch on the desk next to the computer and sat up straighter in her chair.

"Let's start with the shape of his head," the man began, pulling up a screen with a sampling of blank heads for her to choose from. Penelope selected one in the center, and the artist clicked on it. He continued to ask questions, which she answered, and little by little; a face appeared that Penelope recognized.

"I think that's him, at least it's close," Penelope said. "What if I'm not remembering it right?" Her palms were suddenly clammy, and she rubbed them on her thighs.

"You're doing great," the man said. "Just relax and don't focus too hard on one feature or another." He pressed a button and printed out the sketch. He set it down on the table in front of Penelope.

"I think his eyebrows were thinner," Penelope said, pointing at the drawing.

The man waved the mouse and began to reshape the edges of the man's eyebrows on the computer drawing.

"I've always seen people sketching with a pencil in the movies," Penelope said with a quick laugh when they'd finished.

The man shrugged. "Back when I started, that was how we did it. Now it's mostly by computer, but sometimes we do it the old fashioned way, or a combination of the two."

"I'm worried I'll remember him wrong, and the sketch won't be helpful," Penelope admitted. "When I think about what happened, I get a little shaky still."

"That's common for witnesses," the man said with a nod. "I'm sure you did fine. We're all through here; thanks for your time."

He led Penelope back into the main area of the police station, where Nadia sat by herself at one of the desks in the middle of the room.

"Miss Weston?" the artist asked her.

Nadia nodded and stood up.

"When you're ready, I'm back here," he said, pointing at the office Penelope had just left. He shuffled back inside, grabbing a folder from the top of a file cabinet on his way.

Nadia tapped her fingers on her forearms as she watched him go.

Clarissa entered the squad room and took a seat at a nearby desk after a nod at them. She quickly picked up the phone and propped it between her shoulder and her ear.

"Any luck finding your purse yet?" Penelope asked Nadia.

Nadia rolled her eyes. "No. At this point, I think it's walked off. I waited forever to get that bag, and I've only had it for a couple of months."

"That's crazy," Penelope said, fumbling for the right response.

"I know," Nadia huffed. "Joey's downstairs, looking through evidence boxes or something to make sure it didn't get misfiled with another case."

Penelope pinched her lips together. Clarissa hung up the phone and started typing on the keyboard in front of her.

"Does he really think that's what happened?" Penelope asked carefully.

"It could be that, or maybe one of the other people at the restaurant claimed it by mistake, which I find hard to believe. How could you mistake that purse for any other?"

A few notes from a familiar song drifted across the room.

"Hey!" Nadia said, moving toward the sound. "That's my phone!"

Nadia crossed to the middle of the room. Clarissa stopped typing, her fingers hovering above the keyboard, listening.

"That's my phone," Nadia repeated, following the sounds. Clarissa got up from her chair and pulled open her desk drawer. She closed it, moved to the desk closest to hers, and yanked out a metal drawer.

"It's coming from under there," Clarissa said, closing the drawer with a screech. She rolled the office chair away and squatted down, pulling a plain white file box from beneath the desk.

Nadia looked eagerly on as Clarissa pulled off the top of the box. Inside was a stack of mail with a manila envelope on top, addressed to the police station. The phone fell silent inside the envelope, then immediately began ringing again. Nadia reached into the box to grab the envelope, but Clarissa caught her by the wrist and eased her hand away.

"It might not be safe," Clarissa said, eyeing the package. She pulled open the drawers of the desk and riffled through until she found a pair of latex gloves. The phone stopped ringing, then quickly began again.

"Who knows you're here right now?" Clarissa asked over her shoulder.

"No one, just you guys and Arlena," Nadia said. "It's not like I've been in touch with anyone without my phone."

Clarissa picked up the package carefully and tilted it from side to side, testing its weight in her hands. Her expression hardened, and she set the package down, easing a finger beneath the tacked-down flap. She pinched the corner of the envelope and gently tipped it toward the table. Nadia's phone, still encased in its shiny gold cover, spun out onto the table, revolving slowly twice before coming to a stop.

"That's my phone," Nadia said triumphantly. "What's it doing in your mail?"

"Good question." Clarissa stared at the phone, then glanced inside the envelope. She tipped it over again, and a single sheet of paper slid out.

Nadia's mouth fell open when she saw the note on the table. Scrawled in red crayon, written over and over so the letters were angry and jagged, was a message:

"We See You."

Chapter Ten

Just as the sun began to set, Penelope made her way into Joey's apartment building and up the elevator to the top floor. He answered the door, a smile relaxing the tense expression on his face.

"Now I know what they mean by 'a sight for sore eyes,'" Joey said, circling his arms around Penelope's waist and tugging her gently inside. The door swept closed behind them as they kissed in the narrow hallway.

"It's been a strange day," Joey said, leading her by the hand into the spacious main room. One end was anchored by the kitchen, and the other was lined with floor-to-ceiling windows looking out on the skyline.

"It's been a strange couple of days," Penelope said. "Any leads on who mailed Nadia's phone to the police station?"

Joey shook his head. "There's no postmark, so it must have been dropped off or sent through our inter-departmental mail."

"Who would want to threaten her like that?"

"She doesn't seem to have any idea," Joey said, putting his hands on his belt. "The thing is, she's well-known in the tennis world. Athletes have lots of fans and sometimes stalkers. Maybe it's some whacko who wants to make contact with her."

"But her things were in police custody," Penelope said. "That would make it someone who works with you."

"I mean, anything is possible," Joey said. "I'd like to think it's not one of us, though. Hey, take a look at this." Joey pulled his phone from his pocket and began playing a video.

"What is that?" Penelope asked. A rusty barrel roared with flames. She could see several branches sticking out of it, the leaves curling and turning black from the flames. Smoke billowed up into the blue sky behind.

"A trash fire," Joey said. "Keep watching."

From the edge of the screen, Nadia's orange bag that Penelope had admired at Sonya's the day before was tossed on top of a rusty trash barrel roaring with flames. Sticks and branches poked out of the top, and one of the purse straps caught on one. The fire regained its force and engulfed the purse, the flames charring the sides, the leather bubbling and turning black.

Penelope put a hand over her mouth as she watched, transfixed by the fire and the burning bag. Her eyes drifted to the area around the trash barrel, which was sitting in the center of a clearing in a wooded area next to a picnic table.

"This is another threat," Penelope said. "Like the note with the phone. This isn't just some overexcited fan. This person is dangerous. Has Nadia seen this?"

"Not yet. I just saw it for the first time myself before you got here," Joey said, restarting the video from the beginning. "We took Nadia's phone to our techs, and they checked it for tampering, made sure it hadn't been turned into an explosive device. It looks like all of her contact information wiped, photos, things like that. The only thing left was this video."

"Someone is definitely sending a message," Penelope murmured.

Joey sighed and clicked off his phone. "It's possible someone has fixated on Nadia, and their obsession is coming out in unhealthy ways."

"Or it's something more personal," Penelope said. "Were there any fingerprints on the phone? DNA or anything like that?"

"Afraid not," Joey said. "The phone was wiped cleaned with a bleach wipe after they wiped the contents clean."

"So they're being very careful," Penelope said.

"Look, I know the last couple of days have been crazy," Joey said, pocketing his phone.

"Really crazy," Penelope agreed.

"But let's put it aside and enjoy our last evening together before you leave for…how long is it this time?"

"Thirteen weeks, give or take," Penelope said with a sigh.

"That's a lot of time away from each other," Joey said. "First thing in the morning, I'm devoting all my energy to finding whoever did this. But tonight, I want to enjoy time with you."

Penelope nodded, although part of her felt guilty for enjoying herself. "Nadia's at the house with Arlena, and Max is over for the night, too. She's upset, but I know she'll be safe there. No one thought it was a good idea for her to go back to her apartment in the city alone."

"Good thinking," Joey said. "Safety in numbers. Now, speaking of numbers, I made something special for the two of us. A going-away dinner so you'll remember to miss me."

Penelope laughed. "I never forget to miss you when I'm away. That's impossible, no matter what you cook for me."

Joey led her through the main room onto the balcony.

"Wow, it's such a beautiful night," Penelope said. The air was warm, with just a slight breeze that caused the flame to flutter slightly inside the glass hurricane lamp at the center of the table. A few matching candles were placed around the patio, illuminating the patio in a soft glow.

The table was set with white and green plates and bowls and long-stemmed green-tinted wine glasses. "Look at your new plates." She slipped an arm around Joey's waist and leaned up to kiss his cheek. "And glasses, too?"

Joey blushed. "Yeah, I got them a while back and have been saving them for a special night. I wanted something a little nicer than the hand-me-down stuff I got from Ma. I don't know, the lady at the store said these went nice together. What do you think?" He pulled a bottle of white wine from an ice bucket on the side table and poured them each a glass. He put a hand on the small of her back and ushered her to the railing so they could enjoy the view.

"I think she was right," Penelope said. She glanced over her shoulder toward the kitchen, which anchored the main sitting room. "Something smells good in there."

"I hope it turned out okay," Joey said. "My first attempt at *Spaghetti alle Vongole*. I had to call Ma three times with questions."

"Did you get fresh clams?" Penelope asked with a grin.

Joey winked at her and nodded.

"Impressive," Penelope said. "When did you have time to do all this?"

"Turns out, when you have a partner, you don't have to do every single thing on a case. I told Clarissa I'd make it up to her if she handled some extra paperwork so I could head out a little early."

Penelope thought about Clarissa's clenched jaw and the conversation she'd overheard in her back yard. "You sure that will go over well?" Penelope bit her bottom lip, afraid for a moment she'd overstepped.

"Yeah, we've butt heads some, but that's normal with a new partner," Joey said, shrugging. "Anyway, she says she's following up on a couple leads. I don't think she's got anyone to go home to, except maybe her cat."

"She told you about her cat?" Penelope asked.

"No, I'm just guessing."

"Be nice, Joey," Penelope warned.

"Plus, with you out of town, I'll have nothing better to do than work day and night until we catch these guys, so I'll have plenty of time to make it up to her. But tonight, I wasn't going to miss."

Penelope kissed him. "Thanks for making it so special."

"Like I said, I want it to be memorable," Joey said.

"Every time we're together is memorable," Penelope said. "Even when we just order a pizza and watch a movie. Not that I'm complaining about you broadening your culinary horizons."

"My girlfriend is a world-class chef," Joey said. "I have to step up my game to keep up."

Penelope laughed and kissed him again, setting her wine glass on the table and circling her arms around his neck.

A timer went off in the kitchen, and Joey stepped away. "Sit. Enjoy the view. I'll be back."

"Do you need a hand?" Penelope called after him.

"No way," Joey said. "You're leaving tomorrow to cook day and night for weeks. Tonight, you get to relax."

"I could get used to this," Penelope teased, topping off her glass.

"That's what I'm hoping," Joey said.

"What?" Penelope asked, not sure she'd heard him right.

"Nothing," he called from the kitchen. "So, tell me about the rest of your day. Did you get some rest?" Joey pulled a sheet pan from the oven, and the smell of buttery garlic bread wafted out toward the patio.

"It was an okay day," Penelope said. "I didn't do much, just sketched out some sample menus to show the bosses on the set. I looked up food and wine vendors in Vermont. A little pre-work. I went for a long run earlier in the morning downtown and stopped at Sonya's."

"Oh yeah?" Joey picked up the hot loaf of bread a minute too soon with his bare fingers and dropped it quickly back to the countertop. He shook his hand and blew on his fingertips while whispering, "ouch."

"Yeah," Penelope said, pretending not to notice. She dropped her gaze to the table and straightened a fork. "I saw one of your guys at the cafe. He must have been gathering more evidence."

Joey pulled a serrated knife from the butcher block on the countertop next to the oven and turned back around. He carefully picked up the loaf and placed it on a wooden cutting board. "What do you mean one of my guys was there?" he asked distractedly as he eyed the garlic bread. "Which one?"

Penelope leaned a shoulder on the frame of the sliding glass door and watched him slice the bread, stopping herself from suggesting a quicker pull on the knife with each cut. "I don't know. I couldn't see him very well."

Joey set the knife down on the countertop next to the cutting board. "You sure it was this morning?"

"Positive," Penelope said, regretting that she had brought it up. Joey was trying to make this a special night for them, and she'd brought up work again.

Joey shook his head and picked up the knife again. He sawed the bread a bit more forcefully than before. "That's news to me, but that's not too surprising these days."

"I'm sorry, I shouldn't have said anything," Penelope said, stepping inside.

Joey chuckled under his breath. "You're not the problem, Penny Blue. Never you. It's just...you know what? Let's forget about it right now."

"Okay," Penelope said, relieved. She went back to the patio, found his wine glass, and poured him a little more before bringing both glasses inside. She set his down on the island near his cutting board.

"Thanks," Joey said. He put the bread in a basket and folded a cloth napkin over it then picked up his wine. A large sauté pan simmered on the stove behind him. Penelope breathed in the briny scent of the clams and the tang of the white sauce they bathed in. Her mouth began to water.

"It's just that," Joey said, putting his fists on the countertop, "I should be informed when new steps are taken in an investigation that I'm lead on." Joey clenched his teeth, then relaxed. "What time was this again?"

Penelope thought back. "Had to be a little after six. I didn't have my phone with me, but I bought a coffee from Lois just before, and that's when she opens. It was before I saw you at the station." Penelope suddenly remembered something. "Hey, did you question anyone in the train station ticket office? Maybe they saw the boys hop onboard afterwards."

Joey shook his head. "No one fitting either description bought a ticket that morning."

"But they could have just gotten on and paid for one onboard," Penelope said.

"True, and we've questioned the conductors on the departing trains. No one saw them."

Penelope rubbed her chin. "You know, once or twice when we were kids, we fare skipped."

Joey looked at her in mock horror. "Excuse me, you did what?"

Penelope frowned and looked away. "I know, it's bad. But when my friends and I wanted to ride into the city and didn't have enough cash, we'd avoid the conductors and duck into the restroom when we saw him coming from the next car over."

"You little lawbreaker, you," Joey teased.

"Stop," Penelope said. "I'm not proud of it. We were stupid. But maybe that's what those boys did. Avoided buying a ticket by scamming a ride."

Joey eyed her approvingly. "We're supposed to be getting video from the station tomorrow. We'll have a good look and hopefully spot these guys. Now, really, let's get on with our night."

Penelope tried to smile, but the reminder of Sonya being gone kept her from it. Joey went out to the balcony and retrieved their dinner plates. He heaped generous portions of linguine with clam sauce onto both and set them down, admiring his work.

"You know," Joey said, "you could use my new plates anytime you like if we lived together. I'm good at sharing."

Penelope laughed, and her cheeks turned pink. 'I know you are. I'm the only child, the one who never had to share."

"Doesn't show," Joey said, picking up the plates and heading back outside. Penelope followed him and watched him set them down carefully on the table.

"So, what do you think?" Joey asked.

"I think your plating is spot on, and it smells delicious," Penelope said.

"No, I mean about living together." They took their seats and gazed at each other across the table.

"Seriously?" Penelope asked.

"Yeah," Joey said. "We've been dating almost two years. I've been thinking about asking you for a while."

Penelope sighed and looked at her plate. "I don't know, Joey. This place is great, and I really love spending time with you."

"But…," Joey said.

"I just don't know if I'm ready to live together yet. I always said I wouldn't do that unless there was a real commitment, unless I knew it would be forever. I never wanted to be the kind of woman who went from place to place without one of her own."

Joey nodded. "I respect that, Penny. I do. Which is why I was thinking, when my lease is up in a few months, we should start looking for something."

"Looking for what?" Penelope asked.

"A house. For the two of us to share. Together."

Penelope's neck tingled with electricity. "Buy a house together? Really?"

"Yeah," Joey said. "Really."

"You know I'm on the road a lot, Joey," Penelope said. "A house requires upkeep, cleaning, landscaping. With our jobs, the hours we keep…"

"So we look at condos. Nice ones," Joey said.

Penelope smiled. "Right. That's a good idea."

"Wherever we live, I just want us to be together," Joey said. "I want all the minutes with you that are available."

Penelope's gaze wandered over the table, the beautiful place settings, the candlelight glinting from the glassware. "Okay, let's start looking when I get back."

Joey stood and went to her, pulling her from her chair into a kiss. Penelope circled her arms around his neck and felt herself fall a little more in love with him.

"Anything else you want to ask me?" Penelope whispered.

"Yeah," Joey said. "How hungry are you?"

"Starving," Penelope whispered. "I can smell a lot of garlic in there. I hope you don't mind my overly aromatic breath."

Joey laughed as he held her tightly to his chest. "It's going to take a lot more than garlic to keep me away from you."

Chapter Eleven

The next morning, Penelope eased through the kitchen door in the back of her house, not wanting to make too much noise and wake anyone who was still sleeping.

"Good morning," Arlena called softly. She padded into the kitchen, bare feet and hair piled on top of her head in a messy bun.

"You're up."

Zazoo danced around Penelope's feet, and she reached down to scratch behind his ears. "Good morning, stinker."

"He's coming with us on the movie set," Arlena said, smiling down at the little white dog.

"Oh yeah?" Penelope asked.

Arlena yawned and stretched her arms over her head. "Our regular dog sitter is on an overseas trip with her family, visiting her grandmother in Italy, I think she said. And I don't want to board him at the vet."

"Max can't watch him?" Penelope asked.

"Is that Pen?" Max said sleepily as he entered the kitchen from the main hallway.

"It's me," Penelope said, a bit self-conscious that he and Arlena were seeing her just getting home from a night out. Max often stayed the night at the house, and it wasn't the first time she'd gotten home the next morning, but she was still self-conscious about it.

"Yeah, I can't watch the little guy this time," Max said. "You know I would if I could." Zazoo ignored them and gnawed on a plushy toy on his bed.

"Yeah, Max's reality show is back in production, and he's shooting a film at the same time."

Max headed for the coffee maker and grabbed a mug. "A friend of mine from school wrote it. Funny stuff, so I'm helping him out, playing his sidekick. No idea if it will see the light of day, but I said I'd help out."

Arlena was still in her pajamas, and her face was slightly puffy from sleep. "I don't have enough time to interview new dog sitters from the agency. Zazoo is picky. I can't just leave him with just anyone."

Penelope suppressed a smile, thinking Arlena was really the picky one, but she understood why. She was hesitant to bring in new help to the house, a habit she picked up in childhood from her famous dad. A few less-than-savory people had tried to gain access to Randall's life over the years, and there was one instance of him being robbed of some valuable movie memorabilia.

Penelope set her overnight bag on the kitchen floor and followed Max to the coffee maker.

"I assume you had a fun night," Arlena said, pulling a mug down from the cabinet to make a cup of tea.

"Very fun," Penelope said, flicking her eyes at Max's back. "Joey went all out, cooked a gourmet Italian feast. We ate on the balcony overlooking the city."

"So sweet," Arlena sang softly.

"Stop it," Penelope said. "I hated having to leave him this morning, but he wanted to get an early start down at the station, and I have to gear up for this drive." She texted Francis, her executive chef, asking him to give her a call when he was ready to travel. She pulled her wallet from her bag and opened it.

"When are you hitting the road?" Arlena asked.

"I'm getting in touch with my team now. I hope to get the convoy rolling by lunchtime," Penelope said. She pulled out a zipped pouch that hid her credit cards inside her wallet. She performed her normal inventory of her things, reminding herself of what she'd need for the trip: personal and company credit cards, licenses, production permits, and ownership papers on her catering vehicles.

"Where's Nadia?" Penelope asked.

"She's getting dressed upstairs," Max said knowingly.

Penelope paused in her inventory and looked up at him.

"Max is taking her into the city so she can gather her things and get packed for the trip," Arlena said, rolling her eyes at her brother. "And that's it. You're not dating her."

Max had an eye for pretty women and a reputation to match, with at least a baker's dozen of fleeting relationships and romances to his credit.

"I'm heading into the city anyway. I have to get to the set," Max said nonchalantly between sips of coffee.

"That's weird," Penelope said, glancing back down at her wallet.

"Not really," Max said. "I've given lots of people rides before."

"No," Penelope said, shaking her head. "I could have sworn I had some cash in here." Penelope opened up the billfold section of her wallet wider, revealing only the black silky lining.

"You know Nadia and I have a plane to catch this afternoon," Arlena warned her brother. "Don't get any bright ideas about whisking her off to some romantic lunch or anything."

"I've already told you I have work today," Max responded. "No time for romance today."

"You always find plenty of time to get into trouble," Arlena countered.

Penelope half listened to their lighthearted bickering as she looked through the different compartments of her wallet. Suddenly remembering, she tucked her index finger behind her driver's license, feeling for the emergency fifty-dollar bill she kept hidden there. When she found it gone, she dropped her wallet on the counter.

"I've been robbed," Penelope said.

Arlena and Max both stared at her, unspeaking.

"All my cash is gone," Penelope said. "Even my hidden cash."

"Are you sure you didn't spend it?" Arlena asked. "It's been a crazy couple of days. Maybe you forgot."

Penelope shook her head. "I took out forty for brunch. You know I like to pay cash at locally owned places so they don't have to pay the credit card fees. And my emergency cash is gone, too."

"How can that be?" Arlena asked.

Penelope's thoughts went to Nadia's missing bag and the video she'd seen. She pushed the thought away quickly. "You know, I'll check with Joey," Penelope said, lightening her tone. "It's probably just a mistake. Maybe my things didn't all get returned yet."

Arlena looked at her doubtfully. "I'm going to check my things too." She stepped quickly down the hallway to her suite as Penelope and Max stared at her things strewn across the counter.

"What's all this?" Nadia said as she entered the kitchen.

"Oh, it's nothing," Penelope said. "I think I misplaced some cash."

Nadia inexplicably looked around on the floor by her feet.

"You almost ready to go?" Max asked. He tucked his fingers inside his jeans pocket and pulled out a ring of keys.

"Yes," Nadia said. "I called the airline, and they said I can use my passport to board. Thank goodness I left it back at the apartment, and it didn't get destroyed."

Max placed his large hand on her shoulder and squeezed. "Let's go then, shall we?"

Nadia smiled at him. "Sounds good."

"Anytime," Max said with a wink.

"I don't seem to be missing anything," Arlena said, holding her bag in her hands as she reentered the kitchen.

"Good," Penelope said.

"See you at the airport?" Arlena said, watching Max and Nadia heading to the door. They were laughing together quietly about something.

"See you there," Nadia said with a smile.

Arlena watched them go, then shook her head and turned to Penelope. "We'll be in Vermont by six this evening. What about you?"

"Before dark, hopefully," Penelope said.

"Our flight's at one. I had a much less romantic night than you, mostly packing for the trip. I got one of those pet carry-on bags for Zazoo."

Penelope's phone pinged. "That's Francis now." She typed a quick message back to her second in command.

"I wish you'd just fly with us," Arlena said, eyeing her phone. "I'd pay for your ticket, you know. You're on the set because I requested Red Carpet Catering, like I always do. I feel guilty you have to drive all the way to Vermont."

"I like riding with my team," Penelope said, setting down the phone. "We've driven farther than Vermont in the past. Plus, it's good bonding time together before starting a new job, especially when I have a new chef on the team."

"They're lucky to have you," Arlena said.

"I'm lucky to have them. And I don't ask them to do things I wouldn't do myself," Penelope said.

"You inspire such loyalty," Arlena said. "It's one of the things I love about you most."

Chapter Twelve

Penelope headed into town to gather a few items for her journey and to replace the missing cash, plus a bit extra, from her wallet. After stopping at the ATM, she parked in the lot of the police station and turned off her Jeep. She spotted Joey's car in the corner of the lot, and her heart skipped, thinking about the things they talked about the night before. Her and Joey, living together. She rubbed her fingers against her chin, then went inside.

"I didn't expect you this morning," Joey said with a smile as he led her back to his desk. The station was set up with four desks together in the center of the room, lined with glass windowed offices and interview rooms. Clarissa sat at one of the desks facing Joey's, a phone pressed to her ear and the end of a pen between her teeth.

"I know, I was nearby and, well, I guess I have to report something," Penelope said.

Joey's smile was replaced by a look of concern. "What happened?"

Penelope shook her head. "I'm not sure. I know there was almost a hundred dollars in my wallet before the incident at Sonya's."

"Okay," Joey said.

"It's all gone now," Penelope said. "Nothing else is missing from my wallet, but…" Penelope noticed that Clarissa had ended her call and was listening to their conversation.

"Are you sure you didn't spend it? It would be understandable if you forgot," Joey said.

Penelope shook her head. "No, I took out forty of it on the way to Sonya's and didn't see my wallet again until you brought it to the house. And I never got to pay my bill, of course, so it should all be in there."

Clarissa stood up and left her desk, heading toward the elevators. Penelope watched her go without a backward glance.

"I'm thinking it's still here, in the evidence room, maybe?" Penelope said hopefully.

Joey leaned back in his chair and rubbed his freshly shaved chin. "No, I didn't see anything else tagged under your name or any paperwork that would have called for seizing your belongings. You were a witness, not implicated, so there was no need to keep any of the items for a future court case."

"What do you think happened?" Penelope asked.

"It's too soon to say, with Nadia's bag disappearing from a secured crime scene, and now this. I hope it's just a clerical error and not anything criminal," Joey said.

Clarissa strode back to where they were sitting and placed a sheet of paper down in front of Joey. Joey's face flushed red as his eyes traced the column.

"We're going to have to talk about this," Clarissa said. She leaned over and pointed out two places on the sheet where the initials JB had been scrawled in thick black pen.

"What is it?" Penelope asked, craning her neck to see where Clarissa had pointed.

"Evidence log," Joey said darkly.

"You signed out your girlfriend's items on her behalf," Clarissa said, her arms crossed at her chest. "You're the only one attached to the evidence. You signed it in, too."

"So?"

Clarissa leaned back over and slid her finger further down the sheet. "And here, too. I checked this yesterday."

"Yeah, I signed in all the personal items from the crime scene. Including the missing bag. Are you implying I stole it and took it to the woods to burn?" Joey said, raising his voice.

"I'm saying when bending the rules and not following procedure becomes accepted, others will follow. Junior officers, evidence clerks, anyone."

Penelope shrank back in her chair, sorry she'd brought up the missing money in the first place.

"You're out of line," Joey warned. "This is a good unit. Nothing like that is going on."

"We'll see," Clarissa said, turning her back to him and retreating to the elevators. She slapped the button on the wall and stepped inside before the doors were fully opened.

"Where are you going?" Joey raised his voice toward the hallway.

"Property room," Clarissa said evenly. "I'm going to get to the bottom of this."

"I'm sorry," Penelope said after the elevator doors had closed. "I didn't mean to cause any trouble."

Joey sat back down and shook his head. "You didn't," he said finally. He looked down at the copy of the evidence log with his initials filling the columns. "And she's right. Something strange is going on around here."

Chapter Thirteen

Penelope regretted not taking Arlena up on her offer of a first-class plane ticket once or twice while crawling through heavy traffic on the New Jersey Turnpike in her Jeep. Her newest chef, Tama, followed her in their mostly stocked pantry truck. Penelope noticed she kept the same distance from behind her the entire ride, which made Penelope think she'd made the right choice in hiring the young woman. Attention to detail and focus were the traits of a great chef.

"Jeez," Penelope whispered as a sports car raced past them in the left lane, her Jeep rocking slightly in its wake. The driver had to be going close to ninety miles an hour, judging from her own speedometer. She flicked her eyes to the mirror to check on Tama again. The young chef's expression was passively serene behind her reflective sunglasses, her arms stretched to hold onto the large steering wheel of the truck.

Francis and Lewis, the other two members of her team, rode behind Tama in the kitchen truck, which was essentially a high-end food truck with every appliance they would need to work. Penelope and her crew could cook anywhere they were asked to, which came in handy, especially on more rural sets like the one they were traveling to now.

The heavy chemical odors of the city fell away, the light faded, and the temperature dropped as they made their way farther north. By the time they'd crossed over the border into Vermont, Penelope had rolled the windows down, inviting the soft fragrant breeze of the early evening to flow through the Jeep. Her ears popped a few times as the trucks climbed higher, hugging the rocky cliffs as they wound through shrinking highways, eventually ending up on a narrow two-lane road. The sky was a brilliant orange with dashes of blue and purple, a few fluffy clouds a lighter yellow that reminded Penelope of delicate lemon curd. She gazed a moment too long then had to jerk the wheel, swerving back onto her side of the road after crossing the double yellow line. She focused on the road and decided to make something with lemon curd during her stay in Vermont.

The GPS on Penelope's dashboard beeped, and she took a turn onto an even more narrow road, the convoy behind following her lead. They climbed even higher, and then the road leveled off, winding around an open field dotted with black cows, the lush grass at their feet appearing neon in color against their dark legs. They crossed a wooden bridge over a stream, and Penelope tapped her brakes, then stopped as they arrived at a gravel driveway and a wide wooden gate flanked by wild blueberry bushes. Ropes connected to a pulley mechanism swayed in the breeze on both sides of the gate, which looked like it had been painted white many years earlier.

Penelope stepped out of the Jeep and clasped her fingers together, then stretched her arms over her head and bounced lightly on her tingling toes. She waved to Francis and Lewis, who stared out of the windshield of the kitchen truck at her with bleary eyes, the engine idling loudly under the hood. "GPS says this is it," she shouted to them.

"You doing okay?" Penelope asked after walking to the rear pantry truck. Her newest chef, Tama, was the first female chef Penelope had brought onto her young team. Freshly graduated from the same culinary school Penelope had attended, she had volunteered to drive the large box truck alone, even though Francis had offered to join her.

Tama gave Penelope a thumbs-up from behind the steering wheel. "All good, Chef."

Penelope gave her a quick smile. "Okay, let's park and check in with production."

"Sure thing," Tama said, revving the engine.

Back at the wooden gate, Penelope tugged on one of the ropes, pulling with all her might to swing it open. Finding it hard to budge with just her arm strength, she jumped up and hung from the rope, using her body weight. She drifted down, and the gate swung slowly open.

"Need a hand?" Francis yelled, leaning out of the cab door.

"I've got it now, I think," Penelope said, rolling her eyes. "I'll let one of you close it behind us."

The gate open, Penelope hopped back in the Jeep and rumbled over the long rutted drive, small pieces of gravel pinging her undercarriage. A three-story house sat at the far end of the property on the edge of a large lake, the windows glowing warmly in the dusk. Penelope looked out both sides of the Jeep at the surrounding property, judging it to be at least several acres and dotted with a variety of wild-growing trees and bushes. A honey-sweet odor wafted through the windows and Penelope breathed in deeply, feeling relief to be in such a pleasant place after their long drive.

Penelope led her team to the parking area at the back of the house, where they lined their trucks up in a row. The rear of the house was lined with windows, looking into a spacious kitchen with a vegetable garden planted a few yards from the door. Penelope took a few steps toward the plants, noticing the netting surrounding it, presumably to keep animals away.

"Wow, look at this place," Tama said as she gazed up at the kitchen windows. "It's beautiful."

"What's that noise?" Lewis asked, slapping at something on his forearm. "Bugs?"

"That's the sound of nature. Shh," Francis said, tilting his ear toward the water.

"Sounds like bugs to me," Lewis said, looking around quickly.

"Your ears are still buzzing from the road rumbling under the kitchen all day," Francis said, waving him off.

"I hear it too," Tama said faintly.

The house towered toward the darkening sky, the turrets on the top floor making it look like a castle from a storybook. Penelope marveled at how she could already see a scattering of stars, even though the sun was still setting. Penelope listened to the sound of water lapping against the rocky lakeshore and said, "It's so quiet; that's why we can hear everything. No buses or sirens of passing conversations. That's what we're hearing. Nothing."

Penelope couldn't tell if it was exhaustion from the drive or the anticipation of their new movie set, but she had a sudden feeling of serene happiness. A brief thought of giving up life in the city and moving to Vermont flashed across her mind as she and the rest of the catering crew walked across the soft grass and up the steps of the wraparound porch.

"Welcome, young travelers," a man's voice boomed from the shadows. He rocked gently on a bench swing near the back door, his bare toes pushing against the wooden slats. He jotted notes on a steno pad in his lap as they approached. The boards creaked beneath Penelope's boots.

"Hi, we're the set caterers," Penelope said. An animated conversation from inside the house floated through the screen door.

"Cool, we've been expecting you guys," the man said, standing up from the swing. He tucked the pad under his arm and the pencil behind his ear, then pulled off his weathered fisherman's hat and motioned to the screen door. "I'm Thomas Truegood, one of the directors. Writers too...I'm in the middle of working out one of Arlena's scenes. The other half of the Truegood Brother team is in the large sitting room. Go ahead in and let him know you're here. I'll follow you in a bit." He pulled the pencil from his ear and sat back down, squinting at the pad in the darkening light. Penelope and her crew pulled open the screen door and stepped inside the house, the scent of warm apples and cinnamon greeting them.

"Pen!" Arlena said, jumping up from a green wingback chair. Zazoo leapt to the floor from the same chair and scurried over to Penelope, his little body wiggling comically. "You guys made good time."

A man in faded khaki cargo shorts sporting a long grey ponytail rose from the matching chair next to Arlena's.

"Penelope Sutherland, this is Jeremiah Truegood," Arlena said, placing a hand on his burly shoulder.

Penelope bent down and rubbed Zazoo behind the ears, then held her hand out to her new director. "Mr. Truegood. It's a pleasure to finally meet you."

Jeremiah smiled as he admired her face. "We're going to do great things together on this film."

"We just met your brother Thomas on the way in," Penelope said. Her team huddled silently behind her.

"My very talented brother," Jeremiah said with a laugh. He pulled his gaze from Penelope's and focused on the other members of her team. "We're assistant directors, co-writers, and producing partners on every movie. Ours is a family business."

"What's it like working so closely with family?" Tama asked from behind Penelope with her soft voice.

"We're two halves of a whole," Jeremiah said. "Without one, the other would fall. We're lucky our dynamic works and that we've found success as a team."

"Who's the better half?" Tama asked.

Jeremiah threw his head back and choked out a laugh. "Well, I don't know. I'd have to think about that. I like to say we're equals, but he's a slightly better writer than me. And I'm better with negotiations with executives."

Penelope threw a glance over her shoulder at Tama, her lips twisted in a wry smile.

"The Truegood Brothers' most recent movie won the Palme at Cannes last year," Arlena said, her voice tinged with contained excitement. "You've made some important movies."

Jeremiah waved modestly. "And some duds too. But the last one was a hit, as you know. Really, it takes a massive team to build any successful venture. In film, that includes the directors all the way down to the chief bottle washers."

Penelope laughed. "I guess the bottle washing falls to us."

"It does, but not you alone. Thomas and I aren't just making a movie, we like to create a community, a family on each project. We'll all be pitching in everywhere to help each other." Jeremiah's eyes sparkled, and his voice hummed deeply.

"So, we'll switch, and I'll direct a scene, and you'll make canapés one day?" Tama asked with the same whispery tone. Penelope didn't know Tama well enough to know if she was joking or serious. She stepped closer to her young chef and placed a hand on the small of her back, pressing lightly.

"Our newest chef has got a sense of humor, as you can see," Penelope said breezily.

Jeremiah pulled at the whiskers of his graying beard and stared at Tama. Francis shifted his weight, and Lewis cleared his throat, the universal signs of being witness to an uncomfortable encounter. For a man who wasn't large in size, Jeremiah had a looming presence, his demeanor somehow imposing and inviting at the same time.

"You're not here to simply feed the masses between takes. And there will be masses, at least some days. You're here because Arlena believes you're up to the challenge of nurturing our crew, providing our film family with life-sustaining fuel, nourishing our bodies and souls while we embark on this artistic venture together."

Penelope glanced from Jeremiah to Arlena, taking in the expectant looks on their faces. A finger of unease slid down her spine, and she heard Lewis clear his throat again.

"We're capable," Penelope said confidently, despite her unspoken concerns. "And we're able to provide whatever is required to nurture the film family."

Jeremiah eyed them once again, his eyes resting a beat longer than normal on each of them. "That's exactly what I wanted to hear."

"Penelope is the best," Arlena said. "You'll see."

Jeremiah smiled warmly at his leading lady and took her slender hand in his thick, rough one. Penelope noticed his fingernails were rough and bitten to the quick.

"Arlena, I trust you've found your suite upstairs to your liking?"

"It's perfect," Arlena gushed. "And Nadia is in the adjoining room, so it will be easy for us to work together each day after filming."

"Penelope, you and your team will reside in the boat house during the shoot," Jeremiah said, nodding toward the back of the house. The screen door slapped against the frame, and Penelope heard the pad of bare feet approaching the living room.

"The boat house?" Penelope tried to picture what a place like that would look like, only able to imagine the canoe shelters at Central Park, with the ancient docks inside and the water rushing underneath.

"Yes, it's out front on the water. Beautiful place to live," Jeremiah said, motioning toward the lakeside of the house. Penelope looked quickly behind her, then toward what she thought was the front door. Thomas entered the room, then leaned against the doorframe, tapping his pad of paper against his leg.

Jeremiah laughed. "So this is the front around here. The way facing the lake. That's the back door," he said, hooking a thumb at what clearly looked like the front door of any house Penelope had ever seen.

"Right," Penelope said, laughing under her breath. "That's going to take some getting used to."

"You'll get it in no time," Jeremiah said. "Just clear the paths of your previous way of thinking. Anyway, you'll have your own space there, and it's close to the main kitchen. There's also a root cellar here beneath the kitchen. We've put up a bunch of vegetables from the garden."

"Can we utilize the garden?" Penelope asked, excited about the option of having access to the freshest produce possible.

"Oh, we expect you to," Jeremiah said enthusiastically. He squeezed Arlena's hand once more, then gently let it drop. Zazoo sat at Penelope's feet, leaning into her leg, listening to the conversation in the room.

"We'll go over more details when we all meet for our first dinner together this evening, but just to get your thoughts rolling in the right direction, on this film, we're running a green, environmentally respectful set. That's going to impact all of us in lots of ways and alter how many of us are used to working. It will be an adjustment, but worth it to create a set with next to no waste and smaller than normal carbon footprint."

The mounting sense of unease fluttered through Penelope's stomach when she ran through the list of items that might clash with an environmentally friendly set they'd already brought with them from the city.

"I have faith in you all," Jeremiah said, opening his arms to his guests.

"I'll show you to your quarters," Thomas offered from the doorway. He walked over and handed the pad of paper to his brother, pointing briefly at something on the page. They nodded to each other, but said nothing.

Thomas led Penelope and her team back out to the porch, then across the mossy lawn toward the lake. A dock with several boats bobbing alongside it jutted out into the blue-green water. On the left sat a boathouse on stilts, designed to also match the main house, but obviously built many years later.

Thomas shook out his keys and opened the front door, ushering Penelope and her team inside.

"There are two large suites, with two double beds each and their own bathrooms," he said, lifting his long tan arms at each end of the sitting area. His eyes fell on Tama for a second, who had her long, thin arms wrapped around her torso. "Hopefully, it's comfortable. You don't mind sharing, do you?"

Tama gave him a tired smile and shook her head.

Jeremiah lifted his eyes to the ceiling. "Most of the rest of the cast and crew will be staying up at the main house. A few people are going to camp on the grounds. Extras will just meet for the day, so they get one meal on set, no lodging."

"What's the average headcount per day?" Penelope asked.

Thomas rubbed the silver stubble on his cheek. "Eighty people, most days."

"We can handle that number easily," Penelope said, already strategizing the opening day menu in her mind. Jeremiah's comments about running a green set came back to her, and her thoughts shifted.

"Perfect," Thomas said. "I'll get you a list of local farms and approved vendors you can order from. He pulled a set of keys attached to a plastic fob in the shape of Vermont from his jeans and handed them to Penelope.

The sound of a motorboat floated in through the open window. "It's very peaceful here," she finally said.

"It is," Thomas agreed. "Jeremiah and I grew up here. This house has been in our family for generations. I've been all over the world, traveling, working, filming movies. But this is still the most beautiful place on earth to me. And now we get to film here. You can't ask for anything better."

Penelope's chefs murmured to each other, checking out the bedrooms and the modern kitchen anchored at the edge of the sitting room.

"Thank you for inviting us into your home," Penelope said.

"Well, we're family on this set, I'm sure you heard," Thomas said, nodding. "And it's important for us to keep things untouched as much as we can."

Chapter Fourteen

After Thomas reminded her team about dinner and returned to the house, Penelope surveyed her new temporary home. It was a cozy space, but large enough that she thought the four of them would live together for as long as they needed to without colliding too much. Oars that had been decoratively painted with different nautical scenes hung on the walls, and glass bowls filled with sand dollars and seashells sat on top of the main room's coffee table and dotted open spaces in the bookshelves. Sliding glass windows faced the lake and were anchored by two sets of French doors leading out to the front dock, which had two sets of cafe tables and chairs.

Tama opened the French doors and slid out of her chucks, then walked barefoot onto the deck, taking deep breaths of cooling air. Penelope kicked off her shoes also and eyed the boat house's nicely sized kitchen and bookshelves that lined nearly all the walls. There appeared to be at least a hundred novels in the main room and a collection of cookbooks on a taller shelf near the dining area. She peeked inside the first bedroom on the left of the main room and then explored the one on the opposite end.

Penelope counted three kitchens her team had access to: the one in the main house, this one in their quarters, and the mobile food truck. Every film set presented its own set of challenges; a lot of the time, it lack space to work. The biggest challenge on this set was going to be upholding the environmentally friendly requirements laid down by the Truegood brothers.

Francis and Lewis had gone out to her Jeep to retrieve the suitcases. When they got back, they opted to take the suite on the left, leaving Penelope and Tama to share the one on the right. They went inside their room to unpack and clean up for dinner, Lewis already rubbing the sleep from his eyes.

Penelope stepped out onto the balcony and pulled her phone from her back pocket. She sat down heavily on one of the Adirondack chairs facing the water and glanced at Tama. The small girl had hoisted herself onto the narrow railing in the corner, her eyes closed, facing the water. Her legs were crossed, her feet tucked onto her thighs, her palms facing upwards while she lightly rubbed her middle fingers with her thumbs. Penelope watched her for a moment in silence, worried that she might topple backwards onto the deck, or worse, forwards into the water. Penelope had no idea how deep it was under the boat house. She was sure the railing was too thin to balance on. Penelope sighed and looked at her phone, careful not to make a noise and topple Tama over.

A little ring swirled on the screen of Penelope's phone, and no new messages or emails would load. Penelope rolled her eyes, then closed them, easing herself back against the chair.

"No phone service?" Tama's voice floated across the breeze.

Penelope opened her eyes. Tama's remained closed, and she still faced the water in her contemplative pose.

"Um, nope," Penelope said. She set her phone on the table next to her chair. "Doesn't look like there's a signal out here."

"We really are back to nature then," Tama said. Penelope could see a faint smile on her lips. Her sharp shoulder blades looked like a hangar under her soft gray t-shirt.

"There's no TV in there, either," Penelope said. "There's a radio in the kitchen."

"Music is nice, but silence is golden," Tama said, twisting her neck slowly from side to side, keeping her eyes closed. "Quiet helps me concentrate. The less yelling in the kitchen, the more creative I am."

Penelope thought about culinary school days, how the instructors sometimes raised their voices when mistakes were made. She had to admit, it wasn't always easy to perform well under that intense pressure, but she also appreciated her teachers exposing her to what real-life pressure was like. Working as a professional chef wasn't for the weak or timid.

"It's easy to forget how noisy our lives can be," Penelope said, her words caught in a yawn at the end. "Until you come to a place like this."

Tama began to hum quietly under her breath. Penelope's eyes drifted closed and she dozed, following Tama's tune that was somehow familiar, yet too far at the edge of her thoughts to catch onto.

Chapter Fifteen

Penelope and her team climbed the hill an hour or so later to the main house for dinner with the Truegood brothers. Fireflies floated along the path to the kitchen and floated among the plants in the garden. The smell of roasted chicken grew stronger as they got closer to the door. Shadows moved around inside, the low murmur of conversation drifting out into the night, punctuated by jolts of laughter. They stepped inside and were greeted warmly by Jeremiah, who was filling a bucket with ice.

"We don't get a lot of fireflies where I'm from," Lewis said. Jeremiah handed him a bottle of vodka and one of gin and motioned them to follow him to the living room. "That must have been the buzzing I heard earlier," he added as they entered the hallway.

Jeremiah laughed. "I think you might have heard our bees. Fireflies are pretty quiet. But it would be cool if they did buzz, like little light bulbs turning on."

Lewis rushed the words, "I'm pretty sure it was the fireflies. I've heard bees before."

Francis rolled his eyes as they all came to a stop in front of the bar.

Jeremiah set the ice bucket down and stepped behind the carved mahogany wood of the antique piece that Penelope hadn't fully appreciated the first time she was in the room.

"What can I get you?" Jeremiah asked with a twinkle. He had changed into a crisp white dress shirt and jeans. His hair was slicked back, and Penelope could see he was quite handsome beneath his shaggy exterior. "I specialize in vintage cocktails, handed down recipes from my grandmother, in fact."

"Something with vodka," Tama said, taking a step closer. She wore a soft pink halter dress that brushed her fragile legs just above the knees.

"A vodka sling for the lady coming up," Jeremiah said with a flourish. "Wait, are you old enough to drink one of these?"

"She is," Penelope interjected quickly. She didn't want her new employer to think she'd allow underage drinking on her crew. Tama was definitely legal. Barely.

Jeremiah filled a shaker with a dash of sugar and lemon juice, then poured a healthy amount of vodka, shook the silver vessel, then filled a martini glass with the filmy liquid, finishing it with a squeeze of orange peel.

They all agreed it looked and smelled delicious and elected to have the same, except Francis, who decided to stick to beer.

"A Vermont one, though," Jeremiah insisted, handing him a brown bottle from the mini-fridge behind the bar.

Arlena and Nadia entered the room, and Jeremiah made them each a cocktail.

"Where's Thomas?" Penelope asked.

"Making dinner," Jeremiah said, coming around from behind the bar. He clinked glasses with Arlena and stood next to her, sipping from his own glass.

"Can I help?" Penelope asked.

Jeremiah shook his head. "Enjoy a night on us. Your first night in a new place should be enjoyed, don't you think?"

* * *

When they'd finished their drinks, Jeremiah led the group into the dining room, where they took their seats around a long wooden table. The place settings were simple yet elegant, rustic china paired with chunky crystal wine and water glasses. Tapered candles glowed throughout the room, evenly spaced down the center of the table and from sconces on the walls.

"What a pretty table," Penelope said. Nadia smiled at her from across the table where she sat next to Arlena. Jeremiah sat at one end of the table, Tama on one side of him and Francis on the other. The chair at the opposite end was still empty, with Thomas still finishing things in the kitchen.

"You certainly don't look like you've been driving all day," Nadia said from across the table.

Penelope smiled gratefully. "Thanks. Luckily, we had a little time to rest and freshen up before dinner." She glanced down the table at her team. Lewis straightened his silverware on either side of his plate and shook out his napkins a few times before settling it in his lap.

After another minute, Thomas entered from the kitchen with two large platters in his hands. He set them down gently, then turned without a word and headed back through the door. Penelope admired the appetizers, which appeared to be baked brie en croute in a blackberry coulie, chilled shrimp cocktail, and a spinach artichoke dip. Arlena eyed the shrimp nervously. She was highly allergic to shellfish, something Penelope always kept in mind when cooking at home or on any of the sets where they traveled.

An older gentleman Penelope hadn't seen before came through from the kitchen, carrying a plate of vegetables. "Hello, everyone, sorry I'm late. Thomas recruited me into service as punishment for my tardiness."

"Nevan!" Jeremiah said enthusiastically. "We've saved you a seat." He pointed to the one next to Arlena. Once Nevan settled in his chair,

Jeremiah said, "Everyone, this is Nevan Hughes, our on-set historian. He'll be working with each of you to maintain continuity and historical accuracy during the shoot."

Everyone said their hellos as Jeremiah introduced Nevan around the room. Arlena shook Nevan's hand and said, "I'm so pleased to meet you."

"And I you," Nevan said. He shook out his napkin and placed it in his lap. "All of you in fact."

Nevan's cheeks blushed, and he suddenly sneezed, only managing at the last minute to cover his nose with his napkin. "Excuse—" he sneezed sharply again before he could finish talking. After two more barking sneezes, he recovered for a moment.

"I'm so terribly sorry," Nevan wheezed. "Do any of you have a dog?"

Arlena's face blushed. "I do. He's upstairs."

"That explains—" Nevan sneezed again. "That explains things. Excuse me, I'll just pop out to the car and get one of my pills."

Nevan screeched his chair back and walked quickly out the door.

"I'm so sorry," Arlena said.

Jeremiah smiled and propped his elbows on the table, lacing his fingers together. "He'll be fine. Nevan is a pro. He won't let an imagined allergy keep him from an opportunity like ours."

Penelope crossed her arms loosely at her waist and gazed at Jeremiah. "What do you mean imagined allergy?"

Jeremiah chuckled. "Nothing. Just a theory of mine, that if you convince yourself you sneeze when you see dogs, that's what happens."

"He didn't see the dog," Francis said cautiously. "It's upstairs."

"Maybe he heard it then, scurrying around," Jeremiah said, shrugging.

Penelope glanced at the shrimp on the appetizer platter and at Arlena, who had a contemplatively worried expression.

"Arlena could die if she ate that," Penelope said, lifting her chin toward the platter. The room fell silent as everyone focused on the conversation. "Is that all in her head, too?"

"Maybe," Jeremiah said. "I've studied the philosophy of thought. The brain is man's most powerful tool and, at the same time, the most underused asset. There are ways to out-think the things we think are harmful to us."

Penelope scoffed. "Severe allergies are biological, not psychological."

Arlena cleared her throat and caught Penelope's eye. She shook her head very slightly, warning her off the debate. Penelope sighed and blinked at her twice, giving her a small smile.

"But I'm sure what you've studied is very interesting," Penelope added, nodding at her team. Francis studied the appetizer platter, and Lewis gazed out of the windows at the fireflies. Tama stared at Jeremiah, her thin elbow propped on the table, a loose fist propping up her chin as she listened.

Thomas entered the room and stopped abruptly, noticing the lack of conversation among the seven people in the dining room.

"Dig in," he said casually as he took his seat. Nevan came through a few minutes later, his expression a mix of embarrassment and relief.

"Sorry if my dog made you sneeze," Arlena said to him quietly. Conversation had begun again among the seatmates, and the sound of cutlery scraping the plates had replaced the awkward silence of the moments before.

"It's okay," Nevan said. "I'll just have to keep my pills handy. I usually have some with me."

"And I'll make sure my clothes are clean every day and that I don't handle Zazoo before work," Arlena said, nodding. "I can't eat fish, so I know how it feels dealing with an allergy."

Jeremiah looked like he was about to say something until Tama distracted him with a murmured question and a smile.

Penelope slipped her phone from her pants pocket and glanced at it under the table. She could see there was still no service. "Nadia, can you get cell service here?" she whispered across the table.

"Unfortunately, no," Nadia said, sighing. "Thomas says we're in a dead spot. We have to go into town or something to make a call."

"That's going to be rough," Lewis mumbled.

"They have a phone here at the house," Nadia said. "A landline. But no Wi-Fi."

"Wow, no internet for…how long are we here?" Francis asked, a touch of panic in his voice.

"We'll be okay," Penelope said. "There are worse things than being unplugged for a while."

Lewis mumbled something under his breath, then went back to eating.

Thomas took his seat at the head of the table as Jeremiah passed around a platter of salad, butter lettuce dressed and seasoned with oil, salt, and pepper. Various vegetables rimmed the edges of the platter, including sliced tomatoes, cucumbers, and peppers. Thomas passed two bottles of wine around the table from the sideboard.

After everyone had poured some wine, Jeremiah lifted his glass. "A toast, to great beginnings."

"Hear, hear," Arlena said, lifting her glass.

"I'm sorry about the shrimp, Arlena," Thomas said as she served herself some salad. "No one mentioned your allergy." He shot Penelope a glance, then smiled tightly. "I'm embarrassed we served it on your first night here."

Arlena's cheeks reddened in the soft candlelight. "Oh no, it's okay. I can eat around it."

"But you didn't take anything else from that platter," Thomas said. "Even if my brother thinks allergies are made up, please know yours will be taken into consideration."

"Better safe than sorry. I'll go into anaphylactic shock if I come in contact, so it's best if I just avoid it altogether." Arlena took a bite of salad. "I brought my pens, so it's fine."

An awkward silence filled the room as everyone studied their plates or the platter.

"It sounds like we're in for quite an experience the next few weeks," Arlena said, shifting the subject.

"We are," Jeremiah agreed. "What we are undertaking here, with all of your help, will be quite unique."

Penelope set her fork down and took a sip of wine. Glancing from Thomas to Jeremiah, she noticed the brothers shared the same deep-set eyes and easy smile.

"So you've studied Helen Wills?" Nadia asked Nevan, leaning forward in her chair.

"Yes," Nevan said, setting down his fork. "She lived quite a life.

"And that's the life we're here to capture," Jeremiah said. "We'll all be fully immersed in this experience. We're going to be the most authentically prepared crew possible."

Penelope glanced at Francis seated next to her. His expression was wary, but interested.

Nadia nodded enthusiastically. "Yes, very remarkable. I've been reading about her love of the arts. She was friends with Frida Kahlo and Diego Rivera! Not to mention senators, actors, you name it."

Penelope smiled, impressed Nadia had done some research since their initial meeting.

"Yes, that's all true," Nevan said. "Not to mention she was an eight-time Wimbledon champion, a record not broken from her peak in the 1930s until Navratilova in the 90s."

"I noticed from the screenplay that you've shied away from her personal scandals," Nevan said. He pierced a slice of cucumber from his salad and popped it in his mouth.

"I think we covered the events in her life adequately," Thomas said easily. "You know how it is. You can't fit everything into a one-hundred-minute movie."

Nevan smiled politely and pierced a tomato on his plate. "You might have touched on her two failed marriages. Her aloofness was her charm. She was untouchable."

"Hardly a scandal," Jeremiah scoffed.

"It was for the time," Nevan countered.

"This is so interesting," Arlena said. She set down her fork and leaned forward.

"I'm glad you think so," Jeremiah said. Nevan helped himself to more selections from the platter in the center of the table, piling his plate high.

Jeremiah reached his hand over to Penelope and urged her to hold it. She placed her palm lightly on top of his after a moment of hesitation. "And for you and your crew, whatever point in life Helen is at during filming, we'd like for you to match the menu to that time period." He squeezed Penelope's fingers together.

"Wait, you want us to cook like it's the, what 1950s?" Lewis asked. "What did they even eat back then?"

Jeremiah dropped Penelope's hand and laughed. "That's your mission. Not only the food, but how it was made. That way, we can really experience the time, from the inside, moving outward."

Penelope stammered, "We can do that." Her voice cracked a bit, but her gaze held his firmly. "We'll research it."

"There are lots of cookbooks in the boathouse, from every decade you'll need. Hopefully, they will give you some good ideas."

Penelope rubbed her thumb against her palm in her lap, still feeling the impression on her skin from his strong grasp. "I can do some online research, find some articles about how people entertained."

Thomas' fork paused mid-air. "There is a library in town. They have a few computers."

"How far away is that?" Francis asked quickly.

Jeremiah chuckled. "Not too far. Half hour up the road."

Francis visibly deflated in his seat. He finished the wine in his glass, then grabbed the half-full bottle in front of him to refill it.

"That will be an adjustment for us," Penelope said. "We usually do our food ordering, report payroll to production, menu plan, you know…pretty much everything, all online."

Jeremiah leaned back in his chair. "We're production. You'll be submitting handwritten reports like everyone else on the team. And you won't be doing big food orders, having products trucked in from who knows where. Everything you prepare for us will be sourced locally, either out of our garden here or through the local businesses in Micklesburg, or our neighboring local farms. And the lake you'll be sleeping over," he nodded at the windows and the blackness beyond, "has some of the best trout you can catch in the country. You'll have access to the boats and fishing gear."

"Fishing?" Lewis asked. He took another gulp of wine.

"You don't fish?" Jeremiah asked.

"Never in my life," Lewis responded. "I can cook any kind of fish you give me, though."

"Where are you from?" Thomas asked.

"Downtown Baltimore," Lewis said, sitting up taller.

"Some of the best seafood in the country comes from there," Thomas said.

"Not from my neighborhood," Lewis said with a laugh. His eyes were glassy in the light. Penelope couldn't decide if it was from amusement or exhaustion from traveling.

"Okay," Thomas said, raising his arms in the air. "Bright and early, we're going fishing. These young chefs are going to see what it's like to catch what they cook."

"Wait," Penelope said. "We have to get organized, prepare for the rest of the crew arriving."

"Not a problem," Thomas said. "I'll have them back by first light."

"I get seasick," Tama said quietly. "Do I have to go?"

"No, you don't," Penelope said. "Lewis, you and Francis can go fishing. Tama and I will head into Micklesburg and maybe some of the surrounding farms, introduce ourselves."

"Perfect," Jeremiah said. "I like how you think on your feet, Penelope."

Penelope gave him a halfhearted smile and picked up her wine glass.

"You're going to use modern cameras and sound equipment, right?" Arlena asked. "Not antiques." Nervous laughter filled the room.

Jeremiah chuckled. "Yes, state of the art. But, newly designed to be more environmentally friendly. And the boat these guys are going out on is brand new, top of the line."

"That's a relief," Arlena said. She and Nadia shared a glance and laughed.

"I'm not trying to make life hard on any of you," Jeremiah said. "My intention is to capture a mood and translate that to film for the audience to experience."

Penelope continued to watch Arlena and Nadia, who were whispering to one another behind Nadia's napkin. Her eyes continued to wander over to Nevan, who, to her surprise, was gazing at her.

"Have you done this before? Consulting on a movie?" Penelope asked him.

He shook his head. "I'm a professor at the university. Jeremiah contacted me after reading a book I wrote on twentieth-century American sport, tennis in particular. I'm excited to see what a real film set is like."

Penelope looked at the brothers at each end of the table and said, "I can tell already this is going to be a new experience for me, too."

Chapter Sixteen

The next morning, Penelope and Tama drove to the small town of Micklesburg, Vermont, in the Jeep. Thomas had given them general directions and encouraged them to take their time to discover more of the area. As promised, Lewis and Francis had gotten up before dawn and were still out fishing on the lake.

Tama had her eyes closed, and her face tilted toward the sun as they hummed along the road.

"Did you sleep okay?" Penelope asked.

"Yes," Tama replied. "It's so peaceful on the lake."

Penelope hadn't slept as well as she would've liked. Unfamiliar noises and the sound of rushing water from the lake roused her a few times during the night. A loud splash from what must have been a fish jumping out of the water woke her one time. After she'd dozed off, the croaking of a frog woke her yet again. She was convinced the frog was in the room, but then realized it was just outside the open window, which thankfully had a screen. Penelope had gotten up and pulled it closed, shivering slightly. The air had cooled dramatically from the time they'd arrived to when they'd gone to bed. Tama hadn't moved once during the night, lying motionless on her side, only the sounds of very faint breathing coming from beneath her comforter.

"I'm a city girl," Penelope said. "Although I've been spending more time in the country lately with work."

"I'm from upstate New York," Tama said. "I grew up hiking in the woods, vacationing in spots like this. My home town is a lot like here, actually, maybe a few more people. I guess it's what I'm used to."

"You don't miss being able to use your phone?" Penelope asked.

"No," Tama said. She pulled an ancient-looking flip phone from the pocket of her windbreaker. "I only keep one on me so my parents can reach me if there's an emergency."

"You might be the only person under twenty-five I've heard say that," Penelope said, shouting over the wind. They picked up speed as they headed down the steep mountain toward Micklesburg.

Tama shrugged. "I suppose. I just want to be in the kitchen, make the best food I can."

"What do you like to do for fun when you're not working?" Penelope asked.

Tama shrugged and smiled. "I read, hike, enjoy the quiet of nature."

Penelope nodded and slowed the Jeep to take the next turn. "What about friends?"

"We're all busy," Tama said. "Look at me. I'm staying in a remote lake cottage in Vermont. Most of my friends from cooking school got jobs in kitchens, in cities across the country, mostly working long hours."

"But they're home at the end of the day," Penelope said.

"I got the better gig, if you ask me," Tama said confidently.

"I think you did, too. But I might be a little biased."

Penelope pulled into the nearly empty parking lot of a large barn-shaped building with a carved wooden sign over the door that read Micklesburg Market.

Tama slid a dog-eared cookbook from her knapsack and flipped through the glossy pages, some of them sticking together from food residue. "I grabbed this book from the boat house. Looks like it was well-used back in the day. There are a few ideas in here we might want to try...put a modern twist on an old classic. I think it's from the sixties."

Penelope eyed the book. The faded cover featured a woman in an apron holding a tray of deviled eggs. Everything from her dress to the kitchen behind her and the lettering was in different shades of orange.

"Nice find," Penelope said. "Today's goal is to set up the shopping and find out where we can bring product in. In an environmentally friendly way, of course."

Penelope handed Tama a handwritten list she'd jotted that morning in the kitchen over coffee and tucked another one into her jacket pocket as they exited the Jeep.

When Penelope and Tama entered the market, they wandered in opposite directions. Tama headed toward the produce section while Penelope walked to the front of the store. A young girl stood behind the counter, flipping through a magazine behind a display case of energy bars near the register.

"Good morning," Penelope said.

The girl glanced up from the counter. "Morning."

"I'm part of a local filming crew, on the catering team. We might be using your market to stock our kitchen, so it's possible we'll be here quite a bit in the next couple of months."

The girl stared at Penelope, a bored expression on her face. "Filming crew? Nice. Help yourself, I guess."

"So, is there a manager or someone I can talk to?" Penelope asked.

The girl pointed languidly toward the back of the store. "In the office. Dairy section." She looked back down, returning to her magazine.

Penelope strolled toward where the girl had pointed. A wooden door was tucked in the corner. The words "STAFF ONLY" were hand-printed in red marker and taped crookedly. Underneath, someone had scrawled the words "Enter at your own risk" in ballpoint pen, which caused Penelope to chuckle under her breath.

Just behind the door, she heard a man's voice, having a one-sided conversation. Penelope assumed the manager was on the phone and didn't want to interrupt him, so she decided she'd wait for him to finish his call before she knocked. Penelope pulled open a glass refrigerator case door and felt the cool air rush out as she glanced at an unfamiliar milk label on a row of glass bottles. Plucking one out, she studied it closer. The label was a drawing of a black cow in the middle of a green field, the words Hefheiser Farms in scripted type beneath it. Penelope stared at the cow, remembering the green fields and black cows they'd driven past the day before on the way to the lake. She turned the bottle around and nodded, seeing the milk was indeed from a local farm in the town they'd driven through to get to their new set.

"Check off the dairy box," Penelope said. "Can't get more locally sourced than this."

Loud voices from the front of the store startled her, and she looked back toward the register. Two young men were talking loudly to each other, joking about something. The young girl at the register stood up and turned to watch them, her arms crossed at her chest, the same bored look on her face.

Penelope took a few steps closer and saw another young man standing just outside the front door, which was propped open to let in the morning breeze. He was leaning against the frame, his back to the store, a phone held up to his ear. Suddenly, Penelope's vision brightened, and the side of his face seemed to glow. She squinted and took a step, eyeing the boy's jawline as he spoke. A twitch and a smile caused her mind to skip back to the boy outside of Sonya's, their faces melting into one right in front of her eyes.

Penelope sucked in a sharp breath, then another. Her heart began to pound, and she breathed even harder. The floor shifted beneath her feet, and she broke out in a sweat, despite the coolness of the air.

The glass bottle of milk slipped from her hand and shattered on the floor at her feet. The store around her began to spin, then turned to black as Penelope fell, fighting to catch her breath.

Chapter Seventeen

"Chef!" Tama's voice came to her in waves, getting louder as she came to. "Chef," Tama urged. "What happened?"

Penelope focused on the wood floor slats she was now sitting on, the pool of milk at her feet. Her heart was still pounding, but her breath had slowed. She concentrated on filling her lungs slowly, then exhaling as her vision regained focus.

"Chef," Tama said, more panicked this time.

Penelope looked at Tama, then put a hand on her shoulder. She was sitting on the floor, her back pressed to the refrigerator door, and Tama had squatted down next to her.

"What's going on?" A man emerged from the office door and hurried to Penelope. "Are you okay?"

"I'm not sure what happened," Penelope said thickly. "I thought I saw someone I recognized." Her eyes darted to the front of the store, but she couldn't see the door from her seated position.

"Come on, let's get you up," Tama said, lacing her arm behind Penelope and urging her to her feet.

"Yeah, thanks," Penelope said foggily. Tama pulled her to a standing position with the help of the store manager, each of them on one side of her.

When she was back upright, Penelope saw the cashier from the front of the store staring at her from the aisle, with the three boys who were now all inside watching her silently in a loose circle.

"Cheri," the man said gruffly, "stop staring at the lady and help, will you?"

Cheri blushed, and she turned around, ushering the others away from the aisle so Penelope could pass through.

"Do you need an ambulance?" the man asked. He was short and solid, his arm under Penelope's hand thick and muscular.

"No," Penelope said quickly. "I just got dizzy there for a minute. I'll be okay." She shot a glance at the boys who were pretending not to watch her walk to the counter, and a strange, weightless feeling slipped over her again. None of them looked familiar to her; they weren't the boys from the attack at Sonya's. Penelope's cheeks blushed as she pushed down her embarrassment. "Sorry about the milk. I'll pay for it, of course."

The manager waved her off. He was dressed casually in jeans and a flannel shirt. He didn't have a nametag, and Penelope realized she just assumed he was in charge. "It's nothing. I just want to be sure you're okay."

Cheri pulled a wooden stool from behind the counter and offered it to Penelope, who smiled gratefully. Penelope closed her eyes and took a few breaths.

"Okay, we've all seen enough," the man said. "You boys go about your business now."

The three young men shuffled away from the counter, heading further into the store to finish their shopping.

Penelope opened her eyes and smiled weakly at the man. "I'm really sorry."

The man put a burly hand on Penelope's shoulder. "It's nothing. Honestly." Tama looked at her with concern.

"Tama," Penelope said, clearing her throat, "go ahead and get the stuff on the lists. I'm going to rest a bit." She pulled out the one from her pocket and handed it to her.

"Sure," Tama said.

"I'm Penelope Sutherland," she said after Tama had stepped away. "We're staying up at the Truegood house for the next few weeks."

"Oh yeah," the man said. "I heard the Truegoods were in town, making a movie up at the house."

"Right," Penelope said. "So we'll be coming to you for some things. At least a couple times a week. To stock the kitchen. I was hoping we could talk, figure out the best way that will work for both of us."

"Sure," the man said. "We can help with delivery; bring whatever you need up the mountain."

"Oh, that sounds great. I'm sorry," Penelope said. "What was your name?"

"Oh," the man laughed. "Nate Hefheiser. This is my family's store."

Penelope remembered the milk bottle's label. "Are you part of Hefheiser Farm, too?"

"That's us," Nate said, smiling. "Fourth generation dairy farmer, at your service."

"Nice to meet you," Penelope said. She slid a foot down to the floor and tested her strength before rising up to shake his hand. "Sorry to make such a dramatic first impression."

Nate laughed. The lines in his face told her he did that a lot. "There's plenty more where that came from. You know the old saying about spilt milk."

Penelope laughed and rolled her eyes. "I must not have had enough for breakfast. I've never fainted before."

"Let me get you something to eat," Nate said.

"Oh, don't go to any trouble," Penelope said.

"Wait here," Nate said as he turned to go.

"So you're really working on a movie set?" Cheri said from behind the counter. Penelope forgot the girl had been standing there.

Penelope cleared her throat and nodded. Cheri appeared about to say something else but didn't as the boys approached the counter. They took turns laying down items in front of her, similar in their combination of tastes: chips, sodas, and energy drinks. The last young man seemed to linger, smiling shyly at Cheri as she counted out his change. Penelope noticed the other two ribbing him as they left, the back of his neck red from their teasing.

"You know them?" Penelope asked.

"Yeah," Cheri said, shrugging. "From school. But I graduated already."

"And how about Mr. Hefheiser?"

"He's my uncle," Cheri said with another shrug.

"Oh," Penelope said. Cheri seemed to say the fewest words possible, which didn't leave much to work with to sustain a conversation.

"Why did you faint?" Cheri asked suddenly.

"I'm not sure," Penelope said. "I haven't been sleeping well." What she really thought was she'd had some kind of flashback that caused her to panic, something that had never happened to her before.

"Your face went totally white. I was watching you," Cheri said. She turned on her heel abruptly and went to the far end of the counter, where she opened a small box and began to sort through a new stack of magazines.

"Here you go, Mrs. Sutherland," Nate said. He held out a paper plate with a few slices of cheddar cheese and a plum sliced into several pieces. In his hand was a paper cup of what looked like tea. "It's got some natural honey in it. The sugar in the tea and plum will help set you right, if you're feeling faint. Tourists come here to climb and ski our big rocks and mountains all the time, but the elevation can mess with your head if you're not used to it."

"Thank you. I hadn't thought about that," Penelope said, taking the tea from him. "Please call me Penelope. And I'm not a missus." She waved a ring-less hand in the air.

Nate's cheeks reddened, and he chuckled. "Will do, Miss...Penelope." He glanced at Cheri at the other end of the counter. "Cheri, can you get that milk cleaned up, please?"

Cheri's eyes rolled. "Yep."

"Seems like that would've been obvious," Nate said in a low voice to Penelope after Cheri sauntered away.

"How high up are we?" Tama asked as she placed a few items she'd collected on the counter. A handbasket was draped over one of her forearms.

"Mount Mansfield, which isn't too far away, is over four thousand feet," Nate said. "That's our highest."

Penelope remembered her ears popping on the ride up and relaxed a little, deciding her slip and fall might be more environmentally related than mentally.

Tama set the basket on the floor by her feet. "Got everything from the lists, Chef."

Penelope ate the plum and cheese while Nate rang up their items. He carefully placed everything into two cardboard boxes and brought them out to Penelope's Jeep.

"Come by when you're feeling better, and we can talk in more detail," Nate said as Penelope got into the passenger seat.

"Will you be here tomorrow?" Penelope asked.

"I'm always here," Nate said. He put his hand on the hood and held the door open with his other. He leaned in a bit closer. "Well, either here or on the farm. Here's my card." He pulled a slightly wilted business card from his wallet and handed it to her. "Call my cell first so you know where to find me."

Penelope thanked him as he shut her door. Tama backed out of the lot and onto the main road back towards the lake house.

Chapter Eighteen

Penelope and Tama rolled down the two-lane road. Penelope savored the sweetness of the plum she'd eaten at Nate's, the taste lingering on her tongue.

"You feeling better?" Tama asked.

"I think so," Penelope said.

Tama cut her a worried glance before quickly pulling her eyes back to the road. Penelope thought about how she felt at the store, how everything seemed to spin out of control all of a sudden. She didn't believe she'd actually fainted. She hadn't been unconscious at any point. But she had definitely lost control, and she had never felt like that before. Remembering the feeling of not being able to catch her breath brought another wave of panic, and Penelope willed herself to focus on the road ahead.

Penelope opened the glove compartment and pulled out her phone, relieved to see she had at least limited cell service. A list of notifications scrolled onto her screen. She had several missed calls, texts, and voicemails.

"Let's pull over somewhere," Penelope said. "Looks like I need to return some calls."

Tama nodded and, a little over a mile down the road, pulled into an abandoned service station, easing to a stop on the sandy gravel next to the boarded-up building.

Penelope got out and walked to a weathered picnic table. She sat down and put the phone to her ear.

"Penny, I need you to call me when you can." Joey's first message was from the day before, at around three in the afternoon, when she'd been making the drive to Vermont. The next two messages were queries about catering services on upcoming projects, something Penelope was grateful to be getting on a regular basis now. She thought briefly about hiring an assistant, someone to answer her business line, take care of administrative things, and manage their schedule. Red Carpet Catering was building a name for itself, and Penelope was often too busy to answer calls for new jobs. And in this case, she wasn't sure when she'd be able to return calls regularly unless she used the landline at the lake house. Somehow, that felt unprofessional.

Her thoughts were interrupted by another message from Joey, this time his voice more urgent. "Penny, call me," he said simply before hanging up.

The final message from Joey was from early that morning. He sounded tired and ended with, "I need to hear from you. I'm beginning to worry."

Penelope tapped the button to call him back and turned to see where Tama was as the phone rang. She saw her wandering around the property, peeking into the windows of the gas station, squinting at the gaps in the plywood covering the glass.

"There you are," Joey answered, relief clear in his voice.

"I'm here," Penelope said. "In rural Vermont with little to no cell service. We're up closer to town at the moment, but I won't have a phone on location for this job."

Joey blew out a sigh. "That's okay. I'm happy you're there safe. The trip go well?"

Penelope told him about the drive, which was mostly uneventful, and a quick rundown of where they were staying. "There's a phone there. Maybe you can look it up. Next time I'm there, I'll jot it down and text it to you."

"Good. Listen, there's something else I need to ask you," Joey said.

"What's up?" Penelope asked. She pulled off her hoodie and laid it on the table, letting the sun warm her shoulders.

"Can you remember what the man looked like that you saw through the windows in Sonya's place the other morning?"

Penelope put her forehead in her hand and rubbed her temples. "I couldn't see him really well. Why do you ask?"

"Because it wasn't one of our people at the crime scene," Joey said. "Someone went through and looted the place. We're thinking maybe you saw the guy."

"Oh no," Penelope said, sitting up straight on the bench. She thought back to the other morning. "He was wearing a jacket with some kind of reflection strip across the shoulders. He turned his head toward me once or twice, but I looked away so he wouldn't think I was staring at him."

Joey sighed into the phone. "So he was tall, short, thin? Anything?"

"He looked big to me," Penelope said.

"Bigger than me?" Joey asked.

"Yeah, taller and wider. Sonya's got robbed, Joey?"

"Yeah," Joey said. "Whoever this guy was went through the place and took whatever he could get his hands on. Appliances, liquor bottles, you name it. You sure you didn't see the guy's face, Penny? Think for a minute."

Penelope sighed and closed her eyes, trying to picture the man she saw behind the darkened glass. "I'm going to say he was blond, broad-shouldered, with a windbreaker kind of jacket. I wish I hadn't looked away."

"Do you think he saw you?" Joey asked, a tinge of concern in his voice.

"Yes," Penelope said. "But I can't be sure. Wait, there were letters on his jacket too. I thought they were initials for the police or a crime scene unit."

"Can you remember the letters?"

Penelope closed her eyes and thought back to the other morning. "Sorry, no."

"Okay," Joey said. He hid his disappointment well, but Penelope knew he was hoping for a better lead from her. "The robbery and the attack on the restaurant might be related, or it could be the work of an opportunist who knew the place would be closed. An easy target once he got past the police tape."

"I can't believe this," Penelope said. "It's the last thing Sonya's family needs right now."

"We're doing what we can to figure it out," Joey said.

"Have you found out anything new on Nadia's case?" Penelope asked.

"Not really. My partner is running down a few leads," Joey said quickly

"I'm glad you're up there where it's safe, away from all of this," Joey said before hanging up. They finished up their conversation with Penelope, promising to call him the next day.

Chapter Nineteen

When they arrived back at the Truegood property, Penelope saw a circle of people sitting on the lawn, their legs crossed and their eyes closed.

"Looks like a meditation circle," Tama said, her voice tipping up at the end with interest.

In the circle were Arlena and Nadia, Jeremiah and Thomas, and, to Penelope's surprise, her chefs, Francis and Lewis. Jeremiah held Nadia's hand lightly, their knuckles intertwined. Penelope thought she heard the sound of humming coming from the group, then realized it was from the line of trees farther away on the property.

"Hear the bees?" Tama said as they walked up toward the house, boxes of food in their arms. "They like the basswood trees."

Penelope saw a couple of what looked like large brown birdhouses dotting the grass between the trees. "Are those bee houses?"

Tama shielded her eyes from the sun. "I think so. They must collect their own honey."

"If they do, maybe we can use it," Penelope said.

As they passed the group on the grass, Jeremiah's eyes opened, and he smiled at Penelope and Tama.

"Join us," he said, hopping up. He had on his cargo shorts from the previous day and his long hair tied in a ponytail. "We're preparing for our first day by pulling in positive energy."

Penelope looked down at the box of groceries in her arms as Tama set hers on the grass and quickly sat in the circle.

"I'll just take these inside first," Penelope said. Tama's box was mostly canned and dried goods, so she figured it could wait. Penelope climbed the porch steps with hers and set them on the wide kitchen counter in the main house.

She took a peek toward the front door and decided she'd give herself a tour of the kitchen instead of joining the positivity circle, thinking that might be a better way to get prepared for opening day.

She stood in the middle of a large country kitchen, which looked like it had been updated in the past decade, but was still in keeping with the aesthetic of the house. The appliances were of good quality, but not flashy. The countertops were tile, rimmed with solid wood in muted colors. The windows over the sink looked out onto the lake, dock, and boat house. Penelope ran her hands along the grouted tiles as she walked to the refrigerator. She pulled it open, and her eyes fell on a glass bottle of milk, with a green label and trademark black cow. Tears pricked her eyes, and she took a deep breath, recalling the helpless feeling she'd had at Nate's market.

Penelope shook her head from side to side, attempting to fend off a sudden feeling of sadness. She pulled her phone from her pocket and opened the browser. She typed "panic attacks" and watched a circle whirl on the screen, then clicked her phone off in frustration when nothing appeared.

Penelope put the groceries away, then slipped out the back door to the boat house. Once inside, she sat in one of the club chairs in the living room, pulling a blanket around her shoulders and tucking her feet under her as she gazed out at the lake, trying to see across to the distant shoreline.

Chapter Twenty

Penelope's team returned a little while later, rousing her from where she dozed on the chair. She stood up and stretched, her legs aching from being tucked under her for so long.

"How was meditation?" Penelope asked.

They were unusually quiet, and no one seemed to acknowledge her question.

"Guys?" Penelope asked. "What's going on?"

Francis walked over to her as Lewis and Tama went onto the dock and sat down.

"We're supposed to remain quiet for at least twenty minutes for it to work," Francis whispered.

Penelope cracked a smile. "For what to work?"

"The positive attraction," Lewis whispered again.

Penelope laughed aloud. "Okay, I'll talk to you guys when you're done attracting positivity, I guess."

Francis nodded and joined his coworkers on the dock. The three of them closed their eyes and faced the water. Penelope shook her head and headed to the kitchen, pulling open the refrigerator.

"Ah," she cried, jumping back quickly. That morning, there had been eggs, juice, and a package of bacon on the shelf, along with some water. Now, three whole fish were lying on a tray, their frosted-over eyeballs staring up at her. "Looks like we're having trout for dinner."

Someone knocked softly on the front door, and Penelope went to open it. She was surprised to see Nevan, the set historian, on the other side.

"Professor Hughes?" Penelope said.

"Please, call me Nevan. I'm sorry to interrupt, but I wanted to borrow a book Jeremiah said might be here." He wore a tweed jacket with elbow patches and tan pants, looking every inch a New England academic.

"You're not interrupting," Penelope said, showing him inside. "Well," she said, glancing at the French doors, "they're doing some meditation, but still. It's fine. Come in."

"I appreciate it," Nevan said, looking around the room.

"What's the book you're looking for?" Penelope asked. "Maybe I've seen it."

"It's a history of the area. Micklesburg, more specifically," he said as he began to peruse the bookshelves in the living room. "A rare edition, I'm told."

"I haven't seen anything like that," Penelope said. "But we've only been here a little while. Feel free to look."

Nevan nodded and went back to studying the shelves. "So, how are you finding things here? Much different from New Jersey, I imagine."

Penelope paused and looked at him. "Do I have an accent? How did you know we're from Jersey?"

"Not your accent, although I do detect a slight one," Nevan laughed. "I noticed your vehicles have New Jersey license plates."

"Right," Penelope said. "So far, the people here seem nice. It's definitely quieter as a whole up here, much less traffic and people rushing around."

"I expect that's a quite different experience for you," Nevan said. "Busy woman like yourself, a business owner, one who travels all over the states for work."

"Now I know you didn't find those things out by looking at my license plates," Penelope said.

Nevan laughed. "No, I admit, I did a bit of background research on the crew before I came. I like to know who I'm working with." He pulled a book from one of the shelves and flipped it open.

"Even the catering crew?" Penelope asked.

"I'm nothing if not thorough," Nevan said.

"Can I get you something to drink?" Penelope asked.

"Do you have tea?" Nevan asked as he bent at the waist to look at another shelf in the living room.

"I think so," Penelope said as she made her way to the kitchen. She pulled open a few cabinets, searching for tea bags.

"You know, I'm well-versed in Vermont culture and history. If you have any questions about ingredients from the area or popular dishes from the past, please let me know."

Penelope glanced over her shoulder. "I appreciate that. It sounds like something Jeremiah would like, too." She pulled out a dusty box of English Breakfast and put it on the counter. She filled the empty tea kettle from the stove and ran the tap.

"Eureka!" Nevan said, pulling a nondescript brown book from one of the lower shelves.

"You found it?" Penelope asked.

"I did," Nevan said, rubbing the spine with his palm. "Glorious."

"Okay, great," Penelope said. "The kettle is heating up so—"

"You know, I just remembered, I must be going. I promised Thomas I'd look over his pages for tomorrow. We don't want to kick off a shoot with a historical inaccuracy, however small, now do we?"

"Um, I guess not," Penelope said.

"Sorry to have bothered you," Nevan said as he headed toward the door.

"It's no bother, really," Penelope said as she flipped off the burner.

"I'm glad you found what you were looking for. You sure I can't offer you something?"

"You're very kind," Nevan said. "See you in the morning, yes?"

"Bright and early, in the breakfast line," Penelope said. "I'll be the one making the eggs."

A few minutes after Nevan left, Penelope's team came in from the porch.

"Feeling enlightened?" Penelope teased.

"Yes," Tama said. "Namaste."

"Good. I see the light in you, too," Penelope said. "Let's make lunch. I'm starved."

Tama and Lewis took the trout onto the deck to scale and gut the fish while Penelope and Francis pulled together a salad and grated cabbage for some fresh coleslaw. Penelope watched her crew members move together in harmony while they worked, like a choreographed dance, smooth and flowing.

"Maybe there is something to this meditation thing," Penelope mumbled to herself. She tasted the cole slaw they'd made from a cabbage picked from the Truegood garden and decided it was the best she'd had in a very long time.

Chapter Twenty-One

The next morning, after a pared-down breakfast service for the crew they prepared in the main house's kitchen, they all set off for the first day of filming. Penelope and Lewis followed the Truegood brothers in the Jeep, and a convoy of vehicles followed them up the windy road to the principal location. Arlena and Nadia rode together in a black SUV driven by one of the Teamsters. Their location was several miles away, down a road Penelope hadn't noticed the few times she'd passed it. They wound up the side of a rocky mountain, and when they reached the top, they could see the lake far down below.

Penelope had barely slept at all during the night. She had dozed off several times but woke suddenly, feeling disoriented, covered in sweat, and her heart pounding. As Penelope drifted off the second time, she had a vivid dream. She was out front of Sonya's cafe, watching the man move behind the glass, the reflective stripe on his jacket overlaid with odd-shaped letters. She tried calling out to Joey, who was nearby on the sidewalk, close enough to hear her, but somehow didn't. Then suddenly she was alone standing in a crowd, who blocked her view of the windows. When she could finally see the cafe again, Sonya stood behind the fence on the patio, reaching out to her, beckoning Penelope to join her. When Penelope turned to call for Joey again, he was gone, and only the crowd of faceless strangers came toward her. She was rooted to the spot, unable to turn and run from them.

She sat up in bed and sucked in a breath, his gaze drifting to the open window. A cricket chirped on the other side, and something plunked in the water. Penelope was sure she'd heard someone sneeze, but Tama was in the same position on her side, unmoving under her comforter.

Penelope left the bedroom after looking at the clock that glowed blue numbers on the bedside table. She padded to the kitchen in the dark jotted down the letters she saw in her dream, then sat in the club chair again, staring out the French doors into the black night and listening to the ripple of the lake beneath them. Once again, Tama slept through it all, unmoving, still as the night.

"Did you remember to bring the apples from the main pantry?" Penelope asked Lewis. They slowed down to match the pace of Jeremiah's truck. He'd just signaled to take a right, and Penelope followed him up a graveled path. She'd left Tama and Francis behind to start on the lunch prep, for when they returned from the morning's screen test and location scout. More of the actors and crew were due to arrive, and they'd been asked to have something ready. Jeremiah had left instructions for her team on the main house's kitchen counter that morning.

"Yes," Lewis said. "And the peanut butter, energy bars, drinks, craft service stuff."

"Good," Penelope said. "Jeremiah said it's not going to be too long out here this morning. Hopefully, we won't run out of food before they finish."

"I know," Lewis said. "It's not like we can get to the store and back quickly if we do. Not from all the way up here."

Penelope grimaced and peered out the windshield. "Look at this place."

They pulled around and parked next to a series of pavilions with stadium seats enclosed around two brand-new tennis courts and a series of outbuildings. A newly paved parking area edged the impressive park.

"I never would have thought this was all the way up here," Penelope said.

A half dozen crew members were already on site, sweeping leaves from the courts, setting up cameras, and laying down cables in between them and the mobile production trucks.

Penelope hopped out of her Jeep and went to Arlena, who stood with the toes of her tennis shoes on the edge of the nearest tennis court, a worried expression on her face.

"What's up?" Penelope asked.

"Nothing," Arlena said unconvincingly.

"Come on," Penelope said. "I can tell when something's wrong."

Arlena sighed and looked around them to see if anyone was close enough to hear. "It's just…this is the first screen test, where they see what I can do physically. I've never played tennis on camera. Or any sport, for that matter. What if I look like I don't know what I'm doing?"

"But you've played tennis before," Penelope said. "What's the difference?"

"Things look different on film," Arlena said. "After hanging out with Nadia, watching her play…I don't know. I think there's a lot more to it. She moves so fluidly. What if I look like a lumbering dodo bird out there?"

"What?" Penelope asked. She took Arlena's hand and squeezed. "That's not possible. You can be just as graceful. You're going to do great."

Arlena nodded, but the uncertain expression remained on her face. One of the cameramen gave Jeremiah the thumbs up, and Penelope stepped away. "You got this," she said to Arlena quietly over her shoulder.

Penelope helped Lewis set up a folding table with iced-down bottles of water, some trays of energy bars, and a few other healthy snacks. She kept her eye on Arlena, watching Jeremiah confer with her and Nadia on the sidelines. Arlena's shoulders were tight, but her face was more determined with each minute that passed.

Nadia and Arlena took their positions on the court. Arlena mimicked Nadia's wide stance, her muscular legs taut as she bounced on the balls of her feet and spun her tennis racket confidently in her hand, awaiting Arlena's serve.

Arlena hoisted the ball in the air over her head and swung at it as it descended, missing it completely. She laughed nervously and hurried after it as it rolled away from her on the court. Arlena set up again to serve, this time launching the ball squarely into the bottom of the net.

"Fault!" Nadia yelled.

"I know," Arlena groaned. She retrieved the ball again and tried once more to get it over the net. This time, it did, but clipped it on the way over.

"Okay," Jeremiah said, approaching Arlena at the net. Her shoulders sagged further the closer he got. "Try and think about it this way. You're not here on the court. You're serving the ball in your mind only. Visualize being the tennis player you want to be. Think about Helen, what she would have done, and make her moves your own."

Arlena swiped the back of her hand across her cheek and nodded. Jeremiah stepped off the court and stood at the edge as Arlena readied herself for the next serve.

The ball sailed clean over the net and bounced in the center of the opposing box on Nadia's side.

"Got it!" Arlena said.

"That's how it's done," Jeremiah said. "Keep practicing, you two. We'll be taking some test shots, so play as many rounds as you like." Jeremiah touched the back of the cameraman as he passed, the sounds of a tennis ball being thwacked back and forth filling the air. Nadia grunted as she volleyed, but Arlena stayed silent, rigidly concentrating on each return.

"Thanks for this," Jeremiah said as he walked to the craft table where Penelope and Lewis stood. "But I thought I was clear about being a green set. No more plastic at all. I'll let it go today, but I see it again. We're going to find a new crew."

Penelope swallowed, her heart skipping. "Got it," she said.

"And I'd like to see you make granola at the house, not buy the pre-packaged bars," Jeremiah added.

Penelope looked down at water bottles poking through the shaved ice. "Okay," she said, confused. "How would you prefer we do the water?"

"Bring big jugs of lemon, cucumber, and melon water. And we'll re-use glasses that we can wash when we get back to base at the end of the day." He picked up a bottle of diet soda and squinted at the label. "No more of this stuff, either." He shook his head in bewilderment. "What is this even made of? Nothing from nature, that's for sure."

Penelope thought about the kitchens back at the Truegood house. There were two dishwashers, and while nice, they were just the average household kind, not the commercial ones in restaurants that could handle large amounts of dishes daily. "We'll have a lot of cleanup."

Jeremiah smiled. "We have a lot of hands, which will make light work. We'll all help clean up after ourselves. Small price to pay to save our planet, don't you think?"

Penelope thought about everyone from the film set coming in and out of the kitchen, washing their own cups and dishes. "We'll figure out a system," she said, her mind reeling.

"Of course, you will," Jeremiah said as he walked back to the tennis court.

Chapter Twenty-Two

Penelope asked Lewis to get a ride back to the lake house with the rest of the crew so she could make a trip into Micklesburg and visit Nate's store again. She slowed as she approached the abandoned gas station and pulled in, grabbing for her phone in the glove compartment after she parked in the same spot she had the day before.

Joey picked up on the third ring with a quick "Hello."

"So glad to hear your voice," Penelope said.

"You too, Penny," Joey said with a sigh.

"What's wrong?" Penelope asked. "You don't sound like yourself."

Joey hesitated a moment before speaking again. "There's been another incident in downtown Glendale."

Penelope gripped the steering wheel tighter. "What's happened?"

"The coffee shop got robbed last night," Joey said. "After closing. There isn't usually anyone there that time of night, but one of the baristas had stayed behind to do their monthly inventory."

"Oh no," Penelope said, closing her eyes. "Are they okay?"

"I don't know," Joey said. "A kid got knocked in the head. He was able to give the responding officers a vague description of the guy who beat him up. Tall, Hispanic, no facial hair. Didn't recognize him as a regular customer."

Penelope pulled the piece of paper from her pocket. "I remembered something last night."

"What's that?" Joey asked.

"I had some kind of flashback, or a moment of clarity, and I saw the letters on the guy's jacket. I woke up and wrote them down." She smoothed the paper across her thigh and read. "CCCP. I thought it was police initials. I'm pretty sure they were red and white, not blue like the uniforms I've seen."

"I don't know what that is," Joey admitted. "You had a vision?"

"Kind of," Penelope said. "I'm not really sleeping well here, Joey. I'm having more like waking dreams at night, you know? Because I'm not fully asleep."

Joey stayed quiet for a moment on the other end.

"Hello?" Penelope asked, pulling the phone from her ear to be sure they were still connected.

"I'm here," Joey said. "Hang on."

Penelope heard him set the phone down and then heard him typing on a keyboard. A woman's voice, who she eventually recognized as Clarissa, was talking also on what sounded like a phone call near Joey's desk.

"It's nothing of ours," Joey said. "Like I thought."

"Shoot," Penelope said. "Hey, try searching the letters and hockey. The boys obviously played, or are fans. Maybe it's a team thing?"

She heard more typing, and Joey's exhales on the phone. "That's it," he said after a minute. "It might be a hockey team logo."

"What do Russian hockey players have to do with Sonya?"

"I don't know, but I'm going to follow up on this, Penny Blue. Thanks," Joey said. "Real quick, how is everything else?"

Penelope thought about telling him about her episode at Nate's the day before, but decided she wouldn't worry him with it right then. After they said their goodbyes, Penelope scrolled through her emails quickly, started the Jeep, and pulled out of the parking lot.

Chapter Twenty-Three

Penelope drove down a rutted road that was too narrow for her to turn around, which she considered doing, thinking she'd missed the entrance to the Hefheiser farm. She'd stopped by Nate's market in Micklesburg and had been told by Cheri in the fewest words possible that her uncle was at the family farm, which wasn't that far away.

Penelope remembered he'd said to call first, but she didn't mind the drive. She enjoyed the lush scenery and the warm air flowing through the windows, brushing her arms lightly as she listened to music on the radio. She hummed along to a song and watched the fence posts roll by.

She spotted the entrance a few minutes later and pulled in, parking behind a delivery van in front of the barn, the now familiar black and green logo on the side.

"Come on in," Nate said, waving her over to the large red barn. It looked like ones she'd seen on Christmas cards, minus the snow on top. A row of cows was eating hay; their heads stuck through a metal contraption facing a long trough. Penelope breathed in the sweet smell of the hay and the slightly sour smell of farm animals, which wasn't unpleasant.

"Sorry to bother you at the farm," Penelope said. "But I was hoping we could work out a delivery for tomorrow. The rest of the crew is on the way to the set, and we're going to be busy cooking every day after that."

"I'm happy to have visitors up here," Nate said. "Hey, let me show you something." He led her past the row of cows to a series of stable doors in the back. "Look at him."

Penelope peeked over the door into the stall, where a baby calf lay in the hay, its legs bent at the knees under it.

"Wow," Penelope said. "How old?"

"About an hour," Nate said with a chuckle. "My main farmhand isn't feeling well today, so I came down to help this little guy into the world. He's a beauty."

"He sure is," Penelope said. The calf's black hair was shiny, and his eyes bright. He let out a bleat that made Penelope laugh.

Nate grabbed a nearby towel from a hook on the wall and wiped his hands. "Let's go out front. I have an office up there; we can work everything out."

Nate led Penelope back out to the front of the barn and into a small adjoining office. After they were settled, they discussed what Penelope and the crew would need at the house and Jeremiah's particularities when it came to staying green and causing minimal waste.

"Old Jeremiah, he's like that," Nate said.

"You know each other?" Penelope asked.

"Oh yeah, second cousins," Nate said, nodding. He propped an ankle across his knee behind the metal desk and leaned back in his office chair.

"Interesting," Penelope said. "Why didn't he work this out with you then? Or tell me about you directly? He just left me to figure things out on my own."

Nate splayed his fingers and shrugged. "Well, that does sound like him, to be honest. Also, I assume he's busy with the film and all. Jeremiah doesn't always do the logical thing, which I suppose is part of his artistic charm." Nate crooked his fingers in air quotes around the last word.

Penelope shook her head slightly and said. "Okay, then. So let's you and me work out the logistics, and let him create art."

"Sounds perfect," Nate said.

By the time Penelope climbed back in her Jeep and headed toward the lake, she and Nate had come up with a plan for him to deliver whatever they needed food-wise twice a week, or more often if they found it necessary.

"I'll be sure production pays for your gas and whatever delivery charges you want to add to the invoice," Penelope said before she left. "This is a big help that I'm willing to pay for."

Nate waved her off. "I'll charge the regular rate. I learned a long time ago not to mix family and business. It doesn't always pay. And you should keep the details of our arrangement to yourself. That actually might be best."

Penelope looked at him quizzically but agreed. She had learned a lot about family drama in the past couple of years and was finding almost every family had their own history, which was usually best left alone.

Chapter Twenty-Four

Penelope let herself in the kitchen's back door at the main house. She planned to find out what they already had on hand, then add to it with Nate's first delivery. Nate had connections with many of the local farms that sold through his store, and he could provide the rest through Hefheiser.

A woman with grey hair sat at the kitchen table, drinking a cup of tea and nibbling on a strawberry from a plate of fruit in front of her.

"Oh, excuse me," Penelope said. "I didn't know anyone was in here." She placed her knapsack down on the counter and pulled it open, pawing through the contents, looking for a pen.

"Come on in," the woman said. "Do you know what you're making for dinner yet? I'm starving."

Penelope froze and swiveled her neck to look at the woman, whose voice was very familiar.

"Arlena?" Penelope squinted at her and took a few steps closer to the table.

"Ta-da, it's me," Arlena said. She did a small jazz hands motion around her face, which had been layered with latex and makeup that made her appear elderly.

"That's amazing," Penelope said, reaching out a hand, then pulling it back.

"It's so great we could fool you," Arlena said. "What do you think?"

She turned her head from side to side, showing Penelope different angles of her face.

"Well, I recognize those jeans, so if I had a better look I might have figured it out," Penelope said. "But not from that quick of a glance. That's impressive."

"I'm working with the makeup team today. They're testing out some different ages, getting photos of me to show the Truegoods."

"Cool," Penelope said. "I've spent two days figuring out that our main food distributor is their own cousin."

Penelope pulled open the refrigerator and saw a variety of vegetables, and what looked like a row of half a dozen chickens wrapped in parchment paper.

"I wanted to tell you," Arlena said after taking another sip of tea. "I had my agent contact my money guy. They sent a check to Mirabelle, a gift from us to cover whatever they might need. Restaurant expenses, wages, you know."

"Funeral," Penelope said quietly.

Arlena's eyes darkened in her wrinkled face. "Yes, anyway. I hope it helps the family."

"Wait, you said us," Penelope said.

"You and me," Arlena said. "It's our place, so it should come from both of us."

"I'll pay you back," Penelope said.

Arlena waved her off. "You do so much for me every day. Please don't even think about it."

Penelope put her hand on Arlena's shoulder and squeezed. "You're a nice old lady."

Arlena chuckled.

Penelope turned back to the refrigerator. "We're grilling out tonight." She stepped back over to the sink to look at the large charcoal grill on the lawn between the main house and the dock.

"Fun," Arlena said.

"How did the rest of this morning go?" Penelope asked after she'd rooted around in the pantry a few minutes. "You feeling more confident with the tennis now?"

Arlena chewed a red grape. The heavy makeup moved with her skin as her mouth moved, which impressed Penelope even further. "I'm supposed to practice yoga with Nadia, according to Jeremiah. So I can loosen up, become freer in my movements."

"That doesn't sound awful," Penelope said. "You like yoga, right?"

"Not really," Arlena admitted. "I always feel like I'm going to fall asleep."

"Well, maybe Nadia can help improve that. I think it's hard, not sleep-inducing. But relaxing, too," Penelope said, shrugging. She pulled out the chickens and unwrapped them on the counter. "How was lunch? My guys do a good job?"

"I think so," Arlena said quietly. "I'm not sure Jeremiah was happy with all the plastic plates. He said something to Francis, I think."

Penelope sighed and looked out at the boat house. She could see the three of them lounging on the deck, taking their break before dinner prep.

"I understand what he's going for," Penelope said. "We've just never had to work this way."

"You should be working like this on every set." Jeremiah's voice came from the dining room doorway.

Penelope turned, her cheeks brightening. She quickly flipped back through everything they'd said, relieved she hadn't been caught complaining. Jeremiah moved like a cat. She hadn't heard any footsteps or floorboards creaking in the old house before he magically appeared in the kitchen.

"Hollywood is one of our country's biggest polluters. Landscapes destroyed in the name of making movies, not to mention the waste a mass of people create on a daily basis. We're not going to contribute to that in as many ways as we can manage," Jeremiah continued. He walked to the counter and gazed at the chickens Penelope had begun to unwrap. "These chickens came from less than five miles away, dropped off by a friend of the family as a welcome home gift. Wholesome, organic, and delivered in the spirit of community and love. There won't be a better-tasting chicken than that tonight."

Penelope studied the smaller-than-average chickens and admitted they had smooth, clear skin and a healthy color to them. "They are high quality," she said.

"I think you're right about trying to save the planet, Jeremiah," Arlena said. "We should all, every one of us, work on reducing our carbon footprint."

Jeremiah walked to her and took her chin gently in two of his fingers, tilting her face up toward him. For a large man, his movements were elegant, his touch gentle through thick, rough fingers. "The makeup team has done a good job," he murmured, gazing at her face.

Arlena returned his eye contact, staring silently for what felt like an uncomfortable amount of time.

Penelope cleared her throat. "I agree also," she said, turning back to the chickens. "The team and I will work to adjust our methods, switch up the way we've always done things."

"A bad habit is the best kind to break," Jeremiah murmured. He released Arlena's chin and turned to Penelope. "I heard you say something about grilling."

Penelope nodded. "Does that sound like a good idea? It's supposed to be a beautiful evening."

"Yes," Jeremiah said. "We use wood, none of those VOCs are coming from our place through charcoal. I'll show you where everything is."

"VOCs?" Arlena asked.

"Volatile Organic Compounds," Jeremiah said, shaking his head.

"Nasty elements that mess up the environment and cause cancer in humans. Why would people overwhelmingly use charcoal, knowing full well it might kill them?"

Penelope assumed the question was rhetorical and didn't answer. She wasn't sure VOCs were common knowledge either.

Without another word, Jeremiah slipped back to the dining room, his ponytail swinging behind him.

Chapter Twenty-Five

The next morning, Penelope met first thing with Jeremiah and Thomas. The first day with the full crew on location had arrived, and everyone was anxious to get principal filming underway.

"A tent guy has come from Burlington and is installing a large canopy up at the courts, and we'll have one out here on the lawn. Those are the main dining areas, depending on where we have the most people each day. Some days, we'll use both."

Penelope scribbled a few notes on the pad in her lap as the brothers took turns speaking.

"You know the trip up to the courts is about fifteen, twenty minutes from here," Thomas said.

"Yes," Penelope said. She paused. "You guys built the tennis park?"

"We did," Jeremiah said with pride. "Our gift to the town when we're through a brand-new recreation area. I told you, Penelope, we recycle. In all things."

"It makes no sense to disrupt the woods, insert ourselves into Mother Nature for a temporary set, or a bunch of throw-away buildings," Thomas agreed. "I can't stand what some companies have done, ripping up locations and then leaving the scars of their film behind for the local people to deal with."

Penelope nodded with understanding. "I think that's wonderful."

She paused a moment to review her notes. "So we'll be going back and forth a lot, especially with transporting all the dishes coming back to wash…it will be a bit of a math problem to keep both places running at once. Does that make an environmental impact?"

The brothers looked at each other.

"You'll be using gas and emitting carbon on the drives. But throwing away thousands of plastic plates and bottles is far worse. And the water consumption…we had a water recycler installed in the main house that filters and re-uses all the gray water," Jeremiah said.

"That was a good question," Thomas added. "We appreciate you thinking about your actions and asking us when you're not sure."

"Okay, then." Penelope stood up and turned to leave.

Just as she pulled the door open, a production assistant stuck his head in, headphones dangling around his neck, and wires draping down his shoulders.

"What's up?" Thomas asked him.

Penelope got up to leave the small office and allow the PA in.

"Oh, and Penelope," Jeremiah called after her. "It's a big crowd today. Remember, your quest begins now."

Penelope smiled uneasily and stepped out into the hallway. "Quest?" she mumbled under her breath. She looked at her jotted notes, and her head began to spin as she thought about how to get food up and down the mountain, keep everything environmentally friendly, and make sure everyone was taken care of.

Returning to the boat house, Penelope found her crew sitting around the small kitchen table, mugs of coffee in front of them. They fell silent as she entered the room. Penelope was happy to see they were all up and ready and wearing their chef coats, her company logo stitched on their chests. She pulled her own coat on and sat down with them.

"Day one," she said, eyeing them all. "We ready?"

A resounding yes filled the air, and cool relief flowed over Penelope.

She knew she could count on this young group of people, no matter what obstacles faced them. Her job was to make sure the road was as smooth as it could be for them.

Chapter Twenty-Six

A large crowd had gathered around the tennis courts, and production vehicles filled the parking area. Penelope recognized a few of the crew from jobs she had been on before; a couple of the Teamsters stopped by her table as she was setting up to say hello.

They had decided that Lewis and Francis would be their home base crew and run food up from the main kitchen. They had a few hours to get ready for lunch, so Tama and Penelope would work in the tent on site on the salads and side items, all of which they could manage out of their kitchen truck. Penelope ran through the services in her head and felt like it could all actually work.

When they were well underway with prep, Penelope walked to the courts, where the crew was setting up shots, and Nadia and Arlena were practicing playing, lobbing the ball back and forth over the net. Arlena appeared more confident than she had the day before, but her movements were still a bit wooden compared to Nadia's. Penelope crossed her fingers together behind her back and made a wish for Arlena to have a good day on set.

About one hundred extras filled the bleacher seats on either side of the court. Some of them watched the action on the court, shielding the glare with their hands. Others talked to each other in low tones, and a few lounged with their eyes closed, waiting to be called into action.

"We're good to go in ten," Jeremiah boomed from the director's chair on the sidelines of the court.

Arlena propped her racket on the ground as the makeup team approached her, brushes and makeup pallets in hand. The hem of her white pleated skirt hung just above her knees, and she wore a white sleeveless cardigan on top. Her hair was pinned in curls under a vintage sun visor, and she wore dark red lipstick. Penelope was amazed at the transformation from Arlena's modern everyday look to something out of a history book.

Arlena's costar emerged from a nearby tent and sauntered onto the court, passing Nadia as she made her way to Thomas on the sidelines, where they conferred closely, throwing glances at Arlena.

The man playing Phil Neer, the famous tennis player, looked like he'd stepped out of the same history book as Arlena. Dressed in crisp white tennis pants and shirt, his blonde hair was parted dramatically and slicked to his head. He twirled an old-fashioned racket in his hand, then bounced the handle lightly on his palm.

The makeup team finished with Arlena, and she approached the net, sticking out her hand and saying hello to the young actor. Penelope had seen the call sheets for the week and knew he was only around for a day or two; his main role was to shoot this one moment in Helen Wills' life. This movie was Arlena's.

Jeremiah rose from his chair and approached the spectators. "Two minutes, please," he said. "And it's probably obvious, but I will remind you. This is a period movie that takes place well before cell phones and tablets were invented. Please do not have one show up on my tapes."

A murmur of laughter floated through the crowd.

"Also, please," Jeremiah continued, "we have a long day ahead. Books are allowed between takes, but none published since 1935 can show up on screen. You'll get breaks, but if anyone has to leave for any reason, try to do it in between takes. And let someone on the crew know so we can fill your seat and shoot around you to maintain continuity."

The crowd murmured, only a few of them looking apprehensive to continue. Nevan hovered near Jeremiah, surveying the crowd, murmuring a few times to the continuity supervisor, who jotted notes on a legal pad. Penelope's eyes swept the bleachers, and she counted roughly how many were in each section.

"Okay, calling action in one minute," Jeremiah said, returning to his chair. Crew members closed in around him, and the four cameramen swung their lenses toward the court.

Penelope caught Arlena's eye, and she smiled, giving her a thumbs up from the sideline before retreating behind the nearest camera. Arlena returned a nervous smile and shrugged slightly, then steeled herself and turned toward the net.

"And…action!" Jeremiah called.

Arlena and her costar exchanged a few lines at the net, and Jeremiah had them redo the scene several times with interruptions and suggestions in between. Penelope sighed and retreated to the tent with Tama, calculating, as Jeremiah promised, it would be a long day. Some directors got what they wanted in one or two takes, but some, like him, had the actors run through lines almost twenty times. Penelope assumed it was so they'd have their choice, but it could be tedious for everyone involved. After several attempts, the actors took their positions and began playing tennis.

Nadia and Thomas sat at the other edge of the court, watching Arlena closely. Penelope could see Nadia gripping the arm of her chair, her knuckles white. She seemed to jerk each time Arlena returned a volley.

Penelope stood next to the table that held three large water dispensers with lemon, orange, and cucumber slices floating in them, arranging the glasses Jeremiah wanted them to use and reuse on the tablecloth. She assumed he would call a break shortly and wanted to be ready for the rush of a hot and thirsty crowd. She looked again at the spectators, sweeping her eyes across, when suddenly she froze.

A man appeared to be staring straight ahead, not swiveling his head to follow the ball like the others around him. Penelope's first thought was that Jeremiah would call cut, because he didn't seem to be engaged in the action like the other extras around him. She shaded her eyes and took a closer look at him. He was blond and clean-shaven, with a wine-colored stain on his bottom lip.

Suddenly, Penelope's knees went weak, and she reached for the corner of the table. The edges of her vision became fuzzy and grey as the table began to pitch forward. Several of the glasses slipped from the top and shattered on the asphalt below.

"Chef," Tama said urgently. She stood in front of Penelope and grabbed her by the forearms, steadying her.

A bitter taste filled Penelope's mouth, and her breath shortened. She panicked, worrying that she was having another episode like she did at Nate's store. Penelope's head rolled forward, and she closed her eyes, trying to push away the sudden fear that had overtaken her.

"Chef!" Tama shouted, attempting to break through. Penelope shook her head, trying to focus. The water inside the dispensers slopped back and forth, and Penelope focused on the noise, finding the sounds of water soothing.

"Cut," Jeremiah yelled, then looked over at them. "Quiet on the set!" he shouted at them.

Penelope looked over Tama's shoulder back at the faces in the crowd, many of whom were now staring at her. But the man she had seen was gone.

Jeremiah came over to them, the muscles in his neck strained. "What's going on over here?"

Tama released Penelope's arms and stood beside her, a protective palm in the center of her back.

"I think I saw someone I recognized," Penelope said.

"What's she talking about?" Jeremiah asked Tama, who didn't respond, still looking with concern at Penelope.

"Pen," Arlena said, suddenly by her side. "You okay?"

"I saw the man from that day," Penelope said, her voice sounding small and tiny in her ears. "I saw the man from the bus stop at Sonya's. Why is he here?"

Chapter Twenty-Seven

Francis and Lewis got to the location shortly afterwards, and Thomas called lunch. Tama explained to the guys what had happened with Penelope and told them for the first time what she had seen at Nate's store, with Penelope sitting nearby and listening.

"Penelope, a word, please?" Jeremiah said, poking his head into the dining tent.

Penelope followed him outside, then climbed into the mid-sized RV he and Thomas were using as a production office. It had been converted into a mobile screening room, with a bank of monitors in the back and a small desk area toward the front.

"Jeremiah, I am so sorry about before," Penelope said. "The first rule of being on a crew is to not interfere with filming."

Jeremiah sat Penelope down in a chair and pulled one in front of her, sitting directly across. He put his hands out, palms up, and motioned for Penelope to lay her hands on top of his. Penelope hesitated, then followed his lead.

"What's troubling you?" Jeremiah asked quietly. He crooked his thumbs and rubbed the edges of her hands gently. Penelope's first reaction was to pull away, but she resisted the urge.

"I'm really sorry," Penelope said, looking into his eyes.

"You've already apologized. I want to hear what the problem is," Jeremiah said soothingly. The pressure increased from his thumbs, and Penelope was oddly comforted.

Penelope sighed. "I witnessed an incident," she began. "A violent attack a few days ago."

Jeremiah muttered, "Go ahead" quietly.

"I don't know if I'm having flashbacks to it or what. But this is the second time…things keep bringing me back to that moment, that terrifying moment," Penelope said.

"Shh," Jeremiah murmured. "That's totally normal. I wish you would have told me."

"It didn't seem relevant," Penelope shrugged. "It was back in Jersey, and I've never had an experience like the ones I've been having before. I didn't know I'd be this way."

"What way?" Jeremiah asked

"I don't know," Penelope admitted. "Scared. But not really. I just go blank, and I lose control."

Jeremiah stayed quiet and continued to massage her hands.

"I think I saw a man in the crowd on set today that I also saw during the attack I was involved in. He shaved his beard, but I recognized him."

Jeremiah looked at her with a flicker of doubt, then relaxed his expression back to understanding.

"This incident you describe," Jeremiah said. "Were you hurt? Physically?"

"No." Penelope sighed. "We got away."

Jeremiah nodded. "And where are the people who did this terrible thing?"

"They haven't been caught yet," Penelope admitted. "There was another robbery, too. Maybe they're still out there, hurting people." She sucked in a breath and closed her eyes. "We were having brunch at a place we always go, enjoying a beautiful morning, and this guy came in and attacked us—"

"Shh," Jeremiah soothed. Penelope had started talking faster and louder. His closeness was beginning to unnerve her, and she fought the urge to pull away from him.

"Sorry," Penelope said.

"Stop apologizing," Jeremiah said. He put one of her hands in between his larger ones and warmed it between his palms. "This man you recognized today. He was your attacker?"

Penelope looked down at his large hands, hiding her much smaller one. "No. The other man, the one with the beard, he watched us from across the street. I saw him before it happened."

"And why did he cause this reaction in you, do you think? The man was simply standing there." Jeremiah switched hands, giving equal pressure to her other one.

Penelope felt on the verge of tears. "I don't know. Maybe because he was safe outside and he didn't help us?"

"So you're afraid, or angry?" Jeremiah asked.

Penelope bit her inner cheek to stave off a surprising urge to cry.

"He might have just been waiting for the bus," Penelope said quietly. "Why is this happening to me?"

"I would say you're experiencing shock. PTSD," Jeremiah said confidently. "Our brains try and protect us from re-visiting trauma. You witnessed a terrible event. It's normal to feel fear, be concerned for your safety, worry that it might happen again."

Something gave in Penelope's chest, a mixture of relief and helplessness. She'd heard of PTSD, but had only associated it with soldiers returning from war. "I don't want to feel this way anymore," she admitted.

"I know," Jeremiah said. "I can help you cope." He patted her gently on the knee, then stood up.

"Are you a trauma expert?" Penelope asked.

"No, I am an expert on human emotions," Jeremiah said. "Meditation and sustained silence, gifting yourself quiet reflection time will get you through this."

Penelope rubbed her hand on her jeans. "I don't know. I'm not sure how to do that."

"You'll join the morning meditation circle," Jeremiah said. "I'm going to make it mandatory for you."

"Mandatory?" Penelope asked, slightly alarmed.

"Yes," Jeremiah said definitively. He rose and took a seat in front of the monitors, then cued up that morning's takes. Penelope watched Arlena play tennis in fast forward, looking like a cartoon character ricocheting across the screens. "All of us need you to be in one piece, physically and mentally on set. Group meditation will do wonders for you. Trust me."

Penelope looked at the back of his head while he gazed at the screens in front of him. She couldn't figure out what kind of crazy he was, but she was sure she'd never met anyone quite like Jeremiah Truegood. She had to admit his quiet, graceful way of talking to her for the past ten minutes had made her feel more centered. And cared for.

"I'm going to get back out to my team," Penelope said softly. "Thank you for talking with me."

Jeremiah spun around and smiled at her. "Five in the morning tomorrow, we'll welcome the new day together. See you there."

"Okay," Penelope said a bit reluctantly.

As she stepped down from the RV, Penelope decided there was another way to put the incident at Sonya's behind her, to release herself from the anxiety she was feeling. She would figure out who the mystery man was she'd seen twice in two very far apart locations and whether or not he was involved in Sonya's death. Penelope had a feeling justice might work just as well as mindful reflection.

Chapter Twenty-Eight

Penelope set her shoulders straight and took a few deep breaths outside Jeremiah's RV. The air was sweet, and the sun was warm. She took a moment to appreciate that she was okay and safe amongst friends up here on this mountain. She did take a quick look around to see if the blond man was lurking at the edges of the set, but as far as she could tell, he was gone.

Inside the catering tent, Penelope scanned the crowd at the tables inside, the loud murmur of conversation and rumbling laughter comforting.

A row of steam tables was lined up on one side of the tent, with Tama and Lewis in their white chef coats keeping an eye on the cast and crew that came through to serve themselves. Francis moved among the tables, watching diners enjoy the food, and stopping to chat every few feet.

"A well-oiled machine," Penelope said as she scanned the crowd. The man she was sure she'd seen at Sonya's wasn't inside the tent either. Arlena and Nadia were sitting together near the front, picking at the matching salads in front of them. Nadia's phone lay face down on the table next to her bowl.

"How are you feeling?" Arlena asked, waving Penelope over.

"I'm fine now," Penelope reassured her. "I've figured out a plan." She nodded at Nadia's phone. "You getting a signal up here?"

"No," Nadia said, rolling her eyes. "Just took some pictures of the set. Whenever I get a bar or two when we're out and about, I post a few."

"I feel so cut off from everything," Penelope said. "But it's not awful, being unplugged for a while. Now I know what those retreat people are talking about."

"I think it's annoying," Nadia said.

"Nadia was just telling me she's got to go check in somewhere in Burlington," Arlena said. "She's going to spend the whole time she's there online, catching up with all the news."

"Really?" Penelope asked. "Bring us news from the outside world." She flung one leg over the bench and straddled it, facing the two of them. "What's happening in Burlington?"

"Drug test," Nadia said. "That's the closest city with a lab."

"They think you're on drugs?" Penelope asked with surprise. She took a closer look at Nadia's face, with her perfect skin and healthy glow. "That would be hilarious if they knew you back in high school. All you thought about was running, dieting, and training."

"Ha, I know. Remember our big cheat days…Mallomars and black and white movies on your couch on Sunday afternoons?"

"I remember." Penelope laughed. "I can't believe how long ago that seems now. We used to hang out all the time before I went off to culinary school, and you joined up with the youth tennis league."

"Sounds like you both knew what you wanted to do very early," Arlena said.

"I think we both wanted to get out of town," Nadia said. "Penelope was the sister I never got to have back then."

"Same," Penelope said. "How's your wrist?"

"It's fine," Nadia said, bending it back and forth for them. "A deep bruise, luckily."

"That's a relief," Arlena said.

"Well, they're not looking for street drugs, so no need to worry about me," Nadia laughed. "We all get randomly tested for steroids, performance-enhancing stuff. Even in the off-season. There's been a lot of scandals, so it's the league tightening up, trying to catch us off-guard. Wherever you are in the world, you have to report in and get tested."

"That's crazy," Penelope said. "When are you going?"

"I have to be at a lab within twenty-four hours of notification," Nadia said, with a sardonic twist of her lips. "So I should leave shortly. But I'll be back by morning. It's just a couple of hours drive. I figure I may as well stay over, sleep in a quiet hotel room instead of driving back by myself at night. It's dark out here." She picked up a grape tomato and popped it into her mouth, shivering slightly.

"How are you going to get there?" Penelope asked. "I haven't seen too many car rental places in Micklesburg."

Nadia laughed. "Thomas is lending me one of the production SUVs."

"I'd find that so annoying and disruptive," Arlena said. "Are you sure you can't get out of it? I can call someone, tell them you're indispensable at the moment."

"No," Nadia said. "They're pretty strict."

"But what if you were in the middle of the woods somewhere or overseas?" Arlena persisted. "There must be some kind of procedure to get you excused in certain circumstances."

"Nope," Nadia said, shrugging. "The association is crystal clear on the rules, and I can't afford to take a chance on breaking them and get banned from the game."

Arlena shook her head. "Well, just be careful and come back soon. I need you in my corner.

Nadia placed a hand on Arlena's shoulder. "I'm here for you. Promise. And I'm one hundred percent clean. I haven't even taken those painkillers they gave me back home, although I still have my script for them. They'll prick my arm, and I'll turn around and come right back."

"Be safe," Penelope said.

Chapter Twenty-Nine

After lunch, the cast and crew gathered back at the tennis court. Penelope's crew began to break down and clean up. They packed two sheet-pan rack holders that stood as tall as Penelope with trays of dirty dishes and glasses, then spun it around, wrapping it with a wide sheet of cling wrap to keep everything contained inside.

"I hope Jeremiah doesn't see all this plastic," Tama muttered under her breath as they wrapped the second tower.

"Well, I'll have to draw the line there if he does," Penelope said. "We have to get all of this back down the mountain to the house without breakage, wash it, and bring it back in one piece. It's not like we can hold all this in our laps during the drive."

Lewis snickered under his breath at that. He ripped off the last of the wrap, and they wheeled the carts to the pantry truck.

"Use both dishwashers and do whatever else you need to by hand, then get started on dinner prep. We have five hours," Penelope said.

"You coming?" Francis asked as they piled in the truck.

"No," Penelope said. "I'm going to oversee craft service, be up here in case they need anything."

Francis nodded out the window as they pulled away, easing the truck out of the parking lot entrance to make their descent to the house. Penelope watched the tail lights disappear, then turned back to the courts, where she could hear Arlena and her costar thwacking the tennis ball back and forth.

Penelope discreetly scanned the crowd as she straightened a basket of local organic fruit on the table next to the water jugs. The man from the bus stop definitely wasn't in the crowd. Penelope was convinced she hadn't been seeing things, that her mind hadn't put him there to play tricks on her, even though his beard was gone. After a few minutes, Penelope quietly walked away from the table, stepping gingerly, not wanting to ruin two takes in one day. She quickened her pace as she got to the parking area and quickly stepped inside the main production trailer.

"Hello?" she called to the empty mobile office.

Penelope went to a desk against the wall and sat down, sliding open the bottom drawer and pulling out a blank activity and timesheet report. She set it on top of the desk, then eased a metal inbox basket onto her lap and began leafing through the papers inside. She found what she was looking for under a set of completed time cards. Bound together with a black clip was a stack of Extra Release Forms, one for each player that was sitting in the bleachers today, providing background faces for the tennis match.

Penelope undid the clip and began leafing through, glancing at the scrawled names and addresses. After looking through the first half, she paused and sat back in the chair.

"What am I looking for?" she asked herself quietly. "Guy from the bus stop?" She shook her head and began going through them again, slower this time, studying the handwriting as well as the names. She looked for any incomplete forms, maybe one with the address left blank.

When she got to the end, Penelope began at the top again, sorting them into two piles, one with male and the other with female names. She figured she was eliminating maybe half of the options, at least.

When she finished sorting, she went through the men's pile again, reading each name carefully. No one had listed New Jersey as their state, but there were a handful from other ones outside of Vermont: Michigan, Connecticut, New Hampshire, and Rhode Island. The farthest away was a man from Leeds in the United Kingdom, which stood out to her. But in Penelope's experience, tourists would often join a movie for a day as an extra to have a unique experience while traveling. She quickly leafed through the stack of female names and found a matching address and last name, confirming a couple was in town together, probably excited to be behind the scenes of a real American movie.

Penelope re-clipped the forms and sat back in the chair, bouncing the back of it slightly as she thought. Her eyes fell on the satellite phone on the desk, and she picked it up, dialing Joey's number from memory.

When he didn't pick up, she left him a message, telling him about the man she'd seen in the crowd at the bus stop. She ended with, "I don't know what it even means. I just think it's too much of a coincidence. I hope he's not a stalker or, maybe worse, involved with those boys at Sonya's. Okay, I'll call you later. Love you."

The door to the office opened, and Thomas stepped inside. His face was neutral but switched to surprise, or slight irritation, when he saw her sitting at the desk, having just hung up the phone. "What are you doing in here?"

Penelope picked up the blank timesheet and showed him. "Just logging our hours."

"A little early for that. You still have dinner to go." Thomas put his hands on his belt and shrugged.

"Never hurts to get paperwork out of the way," Penelope said, standing up. "I want to keep it with me so I don't have to hunt for it at the end of the night."

Thomas's face relaxed. "That makes sense. You know we're doing dinner up here to save trekking all the extras down to the house."

"That's what the team is getting ready for," Penelope agreed. She brushed past him and left the trailer, with him staring behind her.

Chapter Thirty

That night, Penelope and her crew washed dishes together in the main kitchen. They played the radio and moved to the music, even Tama, who smiled and rolled her eyes as Francis closed his and sang a few high notes of a popular song to her.

"Having a party in here?" Jeremiah asked, smiling from the doorway.

"Is it too loud?" Penelope asked. She reached for the radio on the counter.

"Of course not," Jeremiah said. "Glad to see you enjoying yourselves." He slipped back out of the door and was gone.

When they were done, Penelope went into the dining room to be sure the big table was cleared down for the day. A young man sat with a large sketch pad at the head of the long oak table, scribbling with an ink pen in a series of boxes.

Penelope watched him for a second. "Excuse me."

The artist paused and glanced at Penelope, his black pen hovering over the pad.

"What are you working on?" Penelope asked.

"Storyboarding tomorrow's shoot," he said. He splayed his fingers as if that should be obvious.

"I've only seen that done on computers for my last few jobs," Penelope said.

"That's one way to do it. Or you can be more connected with your art, like this," he said, a slight hint of exasperation in his voice.

"Can you do me a favor?" Penelope asked.

He looked at her curiously. "Maybe. What is it?"

"If I describe someone to you, could you do a sketch of a face?" Penelope asked hopefully.

The young man grinned at her. "Let me guess. You want a picture of Brad Pitt to hang in the kitchen."

Penelope laughed. "No."

"Not Jeremiah," the young man teased.

"Stop it." Penelope laughed, looking nervously over her shoulder for the lurking director.

"Say I do this for you. What's in it for me?" the young man asked her playfully.

"Tell you what. We'll have the crew make your favorite dessert tomorrow, whatever you like," Penelope said.

"Deal," he said, turning over a fresh sheet on his pad. "Peach cobbler. With vanilla ice cream."

"You got it." Penelope took the seat next to him and began describing the man from the bus stop. With and without his long beard.

Chapter Thirty-One

The next morning, Penelope sat on a mat on the dewy lawn next to Tama, shivering slightly and humming along with the circle of people who had gathered for meditation time with Jeremiah. Penelope had finally gotten a good night's sleep, her first since arriving in Vermont. She felt like she needed one or two more to feel completely back to normal, but she wasn't complaining about the good start she'd gotten.

Penelope opened her eyes halfway and snuck a peek at the people around her. Tama's face was serene happiness, as were many of the cast and crew around her. Penelope smelled the wet grass and the pleasant mustiness of the lakeshore, and she had to admit, they did bring a feeling of calmness. The drone of the beehives was gone, this not being the active time of day. Penelope thought this was the quietest the property had been since the moment they'd arrived. Then she wondered if she could make ice cream out of local honey.

"And now we welcome the sun and go forth onto a productive and creative day," Jeremiah rumbled after a few more minutes of quiet meditation. Penelope opened her eyes again and saw orange streaks of the sunrise in the purple morning sky. Several people in the group stood up and hugged each other quickly before setting off to their rooms to get ready for the day.

Penelope started to go back to the boat house, then noticed that

Tama had gone in the other direction. She looked back and saw her talking with Jeremiah. They were laughing about something, his large hand on her bony shoulder.

"Tama, you coming?" Penelope called.

Tama waved. "Be along in a minute."

Penelope hesitated, then turned to go. She took one last glance at the two of them over her shoulder, standing together in the middle of the large lawn, still talking closely, his head bent down to hers.

* * *

Back at the boat house, Penelope stood at the kitchen counter and listened to the coffee pot percolate on the counter. The bedroom door to the guys' room was still closed, but she heard one of them moving around in there. If they weren't up in the next half hour, she'd have to rouse them so they could start getting ready for the long day ahead.

Penelope smoothed the edges of the pair of drawings she gazed at on the counter. She stared at the composite sketches the set artist had drawn for her. His sandy blond hair, close-set eyes, green, she imagined, a long nose and full lips. It was as perfect a likeness as she could imagine, complete with the purple stain on the left side of his bottom lip.

She filled her mug and sat down at the table with her coffee, still staring at the drawings. She sighed and looked up, her gaze falling on the bookshelf lining the far wall. There was one gap where the professor had borrowed the book the other day. The gap in the shelf bothered her for some reason, so she got up to shift the books together so they'd be evenly spaced. When she knelt down to shuffle the books, she saw something glinting from the back of the bookcase. "What in the...?" she murmured. What looked like the top of a mini microphone had been stuck to the back of the bookcase.

"Bringing a book to set today?" Francis said as he came into the kitchen. He'd pulled on his chef pants and a white t-shirt, and his hair was still damp from the shower.

"Um," Penelope said, standing up. "Yeah, maybe." She decided on the spot to watch what she said, and to not mention what looked like a microphone in their main living area.

"Who's this?" Francis asked, looking down at the drawing of the man's face as he made his way to the coffee maker.

"I'm not sure," Penelope said, standing up and joining him at the table. She kept her eyes on the little device behind the books. "A guy I've seen a couple of times."

Francis shrugged and picked up the drawing. "He looks familiar, but like in a general way. He looks like a lot of people, I guess. Especially in Brooklyn." He pointed to the likeness of the man with the beard. "What's that on his lip?"

Penelope felt a prick of doubt in her stomach, then pushed it away. She looked down at the drawing. "I don't know. A birthmark, maybe?"

The front door opened, and Tama came through, a smile on her face.

"Call time is seven," Penelope called after her as she breezed past them into the bedroom.

"I'll be ready," Tama called faintly from the room before shutting the door.

"She's in a good mood," Francis said. He took a sip of coffee from the mug clutched behind his thick knuckles.

Penelope shook her head and sat back down at the table, not sure what to say.

Chapter Thirty-Two

That day's timing and film schedule was very much like the day before. Penelope felt her team fall into their rhythm, which put her mind at ease. Every movie set had its own unique ebbs and flows, its own particular way of doing things. Once they found their groove, it was easier to have successful days. Penelope also kept an eye on the crowd, hoping to catch a glimpse of her mystery man again, but he didn't appear.

After lunch, during the washing up lull before dinner, Penelope decided to drive to the good cell spot and give Joey a call. She told Jeremiah she had to pick up a few things from the market, and he waved her off, unconcerned that her crew was back at the house. "You're doing great today. I told you meditation would work."

"I think you could be right," Penelope said, nodding vigorously. When he turned to go, Penelope hid her smile with her hand. What was the harm in letting him believe it was the meditation alone that had lifted her spirits?

* * *

Penelope entered Nate's market in Micklesburg and looked around for him. When she didn't see him or Cheri up front either, she knocked on the office door. Nate pulled the door open and smiled when he saw

Penelope standing on the other side.

"You're a sight for sore eyes," Nate said.

"Thanks," Penelope said. "I just stopped in to grab a new frying pan. Do you have those? I thought I noticed a housewares section the other day. You know, before I fainted."

Nate chuckled and nodded. "We do. Let me show you."

Penelope followed him to the rear section of the store and chose two new pans.

"And I'll have that first delivery to you this evening. That still okay?" Nate asked.

"Yes," Penelope agreed.

"You know, you could have called to add these to your order," Nate said, leading her back to the front. "Not that I'm complaining about seeing you again."

Penelope's smile faltered slightly. "Thanks, Nate. I was coming through town anyway, so I figured I'd just stop. Also, I wanted to show you this." She pulled the set of drawings from her pocket and unfolded it.

"Who's that?" Nate asked, squinting at the paper in her hand. His flannel shirt sleeve was rolled up, exposing his muscular forearm.

"Someone I've seen a couple of times. I'm trying to figure out who he is," Penelope said, watching his face.

Nate shook his head. "I've never seen him, I don't think."

"I thought since you have one of the only markets in the area," Penelope said, deflating a bit, "that maybe he'd stopped by."

Nate handed the picture back to her. "Sorry."

"It's okay," Penelope said with a sigh. "How much do I owe you?" She held up the pans.

"I'll add it to the bill I bring later; how'd that be?" Nate said, smiling again.

Penelope thanked him and turned to go.

"Would you want to have dinner with me sometime?" Nate called after her.

Penelope turned slowly on her heel and smiled at him. "Dinner would be nice, Nate. But…I have a boyfriend back home in New Jersey."

"Well, I just meant dinner, nothing else," Nate said, his smiling expression unchanged. "You have to eat, right?"

"Yeah," Penelope said carefully.

"Anyway, I'll see you up at the house." Nate waved her off and turned back toward his office. Penelope glanced at the abandoned register, then at the empty parking lot. A gust of wind brushed her neck, and she shivered, then stepped out into the sunshine.

Chapter Thirty-Three

Penelope pulled into the lot of the abandoned service station and put her Jeep in park, cutting the motor. She got out and stretched her legs after retrieving her cell phone from the glove compartment and turning it on as she headed to her picnic table.

Joey picked up on the second ring. "Penelope?"

"Hey," she said. "How are you?"

"Better now that I'm talking to you," he said. Not much had changed since she'd spoken to him the last time. They were still trying to find the accomplice from the attack at Sonya's, and no new leads had turned up in the robbery at Lois's coffee shop.

"What about those letters I gave you? The ones from the jacket."

"It's a pretty popular team, it turns out," Joey said. "So it didn't narrow the field by much." She could hear him rifling through paper, and she pictured him at his desk.

"Sorry it wasn't more helpful," Penelope said.

"Well, CCCP was a popular team back in the 90s, according to my research, so it could be someone older than the kids in the attack at Sonya's."

"Or someone of any age who is just a fan of the team," Penelope said.

"Yeah, like you and your Beatles t-shirt," Joey said.

"Right, like a tribute, something that stands the test of time," Penelope said.

"Anyways," Joey said. "I'm taking a ride to the community center in a few minutes. There's a youth hockey coach there. Maybe he knows these kids."

"That's a good idea," Penelope said. "Call you when I can, okay?"

"Looking forward to it."

Penelope hung up and stared at the phone in her lap. She picked it up and Googled Lois's coffee shop in Glendale, dialing the number.

"Glendale Grind," a young voice answered after the first ring.

"Hello, may I speak with Lois, please?" Penelope asked.

The girl clunked the phone on the counter without a word and shouted Lois's name. Penelope could hear voices in the background and music playing while she waited.

"Who is this?" the girl suddenly asked.

"Penelope Sutherland."

The phone clunked on the counter again, and Penelope sighed.

"Okay, she's here for you," the girl said. The sound of the phone being jostled between hands caused Penelope to pull her phone from her ear.

"Penelope," Lois said. "I thought you were traveling. What's the matter?"

"Nothing, Lois," Penelope said. "I heard what happened at the shop and wanted to check in with you."

The older woman sighed heavily over the phone. "Hang on a minute." Penelope heard a door close, and the background noise fall away. "Now I can hear you, back here in the office."

"Are you okay?" Penelope asked.

"So sweet of you to call, dear," Lois said. "I tell you, it's been a real rough week for the Letourneaus. Real tough. Some guy comes in here, whacks one of my kids on the head, and cleans out the register. Thank goodness he couldn't crack the safe. I'd be in a real jam, then."

"I'm sorry to hear that, Lois," Penelope said. "I'm glad you're okay."

"Thanks, dear. How's the new job going?" Lois asked.

"It's fine," Penelope said. "Quiet. Green. Lois, you said it's been a rough week for the Letourneaus...is that your last name?"

"Yes," Lois said. "I thought you knew that. Why do you ask?"

"I might have met someone from your family the other day at the hospital. The wife of one of the men who was attacked. Her name was Kelly."

"That's my daughter-in-law," Lois said. "Like I said, a rough week. First, she and my son are caught up in the mess down at Sonya's, and now this happens to me. What are the odds?"

Penelope sat quietly for a moment, thinking about what Lois said.

"You still there, dear?"

"Yeah, sorry. I didn't realize that was your family there on the patio with us," Penelope said.

"How do you think I knew how brave you were?" Lois asked. "I heard firsthand what happened."

"Right," Penelope said. "I assumed you had read about it in the paper. Anyway, I'm glad you're okay, Lois."

"You too, dear," Lois said. "I'm glad you're okay too."

After they hung up, she sent Joey a text: Robbery Connection: Letourneau victims at both.

Penelope let the phone drop between her knees and dangle loosely in her hand. She looked at the wood covering the service station windows and wondered how the place used to look, imagining fresh paint and sparkling glass. There was a raised concrete island where she assumed gas pumps used to stand. The roof looked like it would have to be replaced before any other business could move in there. Penelope wondered what it was like to open a brand-new business, then slowly watch it decline year after year until nothing could be done but to board it up and hope the elements didn't tear it completely down.

Chapter Thirty-Four

Penelope was jolted awake the next morning by a rapid knocking on the front door of the boat house.

"Meditation circle," a man's voice called. "Fifteen minutes."

Penelope swung her legs over the side of the bed and sighed. To her surprise, Tama wasn't in her bed, sleeping silently like always. She'd gone to sleep the night before earlier than the others, who had decided to sit on the deck, drink a couple of beers, and talk before bed.

"Early bird gets the worm," Penelope mumbled as she pulled on her yoga clothes. Stepping into the main room of the boat house, she remembered the shiny button she'd seen the day before on the bookshelf and bent down to see what it was. The books appeared untouched, but the object was gone. Penelope rubbed her eyes and pulled her hair into a ponytail, wondering not for the first time if she actually was seeing things after all.

Tama was in her usual spot on her yoga mat in the circle, and Penelope took a seat next to her without saying anything.

"Welcome," Jeremiah said, grasping Penelope's hands in his and shaking them.

"Morning," Penelope said groggily. She decided she'd talk to him later about making crack-of-dawn meditation sessions optional going forward. Penelope had finally found a way to sleep at the boat house and wanted to get more of it now that she could.

Jeremiah walked in front of everyone in the circle, pausing occasionally to lightly touch someone's shoulder or hover his hand briefly over their head. Penelope cut a glance at Tama again and saw she was watching Jeremiah too. Her smile was one of serenity and something else Penelope hadn't seen before. Pride, maybe?

"You're here early," Penelope whispered to Tama.

"I wanted to get a head start on this great day," Tama said, closing her eyes again.

Penelope rolled hers slightly, then followed suit, listening for the soothing suggestions Jeremiah began giving from his place across from them.

* * *

After meditation, Penelope met with her team in the main kitchen. They worked out the menu and responsibilities for the day. Principal filming was going to be in the house that morning and afternoon, which was a relief to Penelope. Not having to transport everything back and forth four times would make the day much easier. She stifled a yawn as she handed out the *mise en place* assignments. They'd decided to grill flank steak and trout for lunch, then create their spin on a customizable fajita station. Dinner would be roasted local duck with scalloped potatoes, yams, or rice, and their standard massive salad bar for both meals. This was their most ambitious meal on the shoot yet, but with the extra time, Penelope knew they could pull it off well.

"And peach cobbler for dessert," Penelope said, remembering her promise to the young artist. "Hefheiser is bringing a bushel of peaches and some of their ice cream from the farm."

The delight in their faces told Penelope she employed a trio of foodies who got as excited about great ingredients as she did.

After they got started, Penelope ducked upstairs to check on Arlena, who was in makeup getting transformed into older Helen Wills. She had to admit, she wanted to stay and watch for a while, but she knew she didn't really have the time. A quick peek would be okay.

As she mounted the main staircase, she buttoned the top of her chef coat. She reached the top and was almost tipped backwards by Thomas, who rushed around the corner and collided with her.

"Penelope," Thomas said. "Are you okay?"

"Yeah," Penelope said, still startled. "What's going on?"

Thomas shook his head. "There's been an accident. Nadia wrecked the SUV. It's totaled. I have to go deal with it now."

"Is Nadia okay?" Penelope asked, her voice louder than normal.

"She's a little shaken up, but she's fine physically," he said. "Some jerk ran her off the road this morning on her way back. She hit a guardrail, almost went down a ravine."

Penelope put a hand over her mouth. "I'm so glad she's not hurt again."

"Me too," Thomas said with a worried grimace. "Again?"

Penelope waived off her comment. "A thing from before we got here. What about the other driver?"

"They never even stopped," Thomas said. "Nadia said he kept going, left her there on a deserted mountain road with a car she can't drive. Luckily, she had her phone with her and was able to call the cops. Obviously, whoever did it was from far away. Folks around here wouldn't leave someone on the side of the road."

Penelope looked at him curiously. She was confident she'd never be able to vouch for everyone in Glendale to act correctly, no matter how much she liked her town. "Let me know if I can do anything to help," Penelope said. Even as she said it, she wasn't sure how she could help.

"Sure." Thomas continued down the stairs, shaking his head as he went.

When Penelope got to the second-floor landing, she looked out the front windows and watched Thomas get in his car and head down the driveway. She pulled her phone from her pocket and looked at the words "no signal," then made a note to call Nadia when she they were out on the road again.

"Did you hear about Nadia?" Penelope asked when she stuck her head into the guest room that had been assigned to the makeup team. Arlena sat in a chair in front of a large mirror rimmed by soft light bulbs.

"Yes." Arlena sighed. "I knew she should have skipped that drug test thing." Arlena glanced at the older woman applying makeup to her nose. The woman nodded in understanding. Penelope assumed it was some kind of shared code to keep what they said to themselves.

"It didn't sound like she could," Penelope said. "I'm afraid someone is trying to hurt her on purpose." She watched the makeup woman's fingers pause briefly before pressing the edges of a latex nose onto Arlena's face, transforming her instantly, but subtly, into someone different.

"What do you mean?" Arlena asked after the latex had a moment to set.

"Well, she was attacked at Sonya's. Not everyone got hit by that guy," Penelope offered. The makeup artist flicked her kohl-rimmed eyes to Penelope's in the mirror.

"She wouldn't give up her purse," Arlena said, tilting her head from side to side to admire her new nose.

"Her bag was stolen from the police station," Penelope said more urgently. "And now a hit and run. Doesn't that sound like a lot for one person in a week's time?"

Arlena nodded slowly. "Or a particularly bad stroke of luck. All those things could be random coincidences. I don't see an obvious connection. And the car accident happened here, not in New Jersey."

Penelope thought about the scrawled note, the implied threat Nadia received. "I think there's something else going on."

"Can you give us a minute?" Arlena asked the makeup artist, who was now openly staring at Penelope. She nodded and stepped outside the door, leaving it slightly ajar. "Okay, I believe you. What can we do, besides let production know? Call the police?"

Penelope chewed her lip and looked in the mirror. "I suppose, but you're skeptical, so they will be too."

The sound of a large truck rumbling up the driveway drifted through the open window. Penelope peeked outside.

"My delivery is here," Penelope said with a sigh. "Let me think about it for a while. I'll see you downstairs."

"Okay," Arlena said. "I'll be in this chair for two hours at least if you need me. Can you send her back in?"

"Sure. You want me to send up some tea?" Penelope asked.

"No thanks," Arlena said. The makeup artist, who had obviously been listening right outside the door, stepped back inside and continued to work, moving in front of Arlena's chair.

Chapter Thirty-Five

Penelope was surprised to see Cheri step down from the truck's cabin and walk to the house with a stack of papers in her hand. The truck wasn't huge, but still big enough that it would take some skill to drive.

"Hey there, Cheri," Penelope said.

"Hi," the girl replied. She handed Penelope the invoices. "Got your stuff."

"Great," Penelope said. Lewis and Francis came down the porch steps and headed toward the back of the truck.

"Everything inside is yours," Cheri called after them. "I just drive, I don't deliver, so…"

"We can manage," Penelope said. "You want some coffee?"

Cheri looked past her at the house. "Yeah."

"Great," Penelope said, turning to lead the way. "Follow me."

In the kitchen, Cheri sat at the corner table, looking around the large space, seeming to catalog the items in the room.

"Where's Nate?" Penelope asked.

Cheri gazed at her and said, "Farm today. Everyone is sick."

Penelope set a mug of coffee down in front of her on the table. A set of loud footsteps trampled the ceiling above them, and a conversation between a few members of the crew was muffled on the other side of the door.

"I'm sorry to hear that," Penelope said. "How are you doing?"

Cheri shrugged. "Fine, I guess. Store's closed, so I can be up here."

"We do appreciate it," Penelope said. She leaned against the counter by the sink and studied the girl's face.

Lewis pushed through the door with a stack of boxes in his arms, plunking them down on the counter. He shook out his shoulders, then went back out.

"Nate said to say hi," Cheri said, taking a sip of coffee and staring at Penelope. "Said to give you his best."

Penelope nodded. "Hey, Cheri. How long have you lived here?"

"All my life," Cheri said.

"And you work full-time at the market?" Penelope asked.

"Yep," Cheri said. She stared at her mug. "I like it there."

Penelope pulled the folded-up sketch from her back pocket and unfolded it. She hesitated, then walked to the table, holding it out to Cheri.

"Have you ever seen this man before?" Penelope asked.

Francis came through next with a crate full of vanilla ice cream containers. He set them down on the floor next to the freezer.

"Cold!" he said, rubbing his arms.

"Yeah, I've seen him," Cheri said. She set the picture down on the table and went back to her coffee. She eyed Francis as he shivered nearby.

"Where?" Penelope asked.

"At the store," Cheri said, shrugging. "I remember his lip thing."

Penelope felt a tingle on the back of her neck. "When did you see him?"

"Last month," Cheri said after thinking for a moment. "Yeah, first Tuesday."

Penelope gazed at the sketch and then back at Cheri. "Last month?"

Cheri nodded. "Yep."

"Beard or no beard?" Penelope asked, pointing at the two images.

"No beard," Cheri said with certainty.

Penelope sighed. So, her mystery man was a local, after all. And the guy she saw a few days earlier at the bus stop was someone else, probably. Someone her frightened mind had overlapped or someone she'd seen while traumatized.

"Thanks, Cheri," Penelope said.

"No problem. Thanks for the coffee." Cheri stood up without another word and headed out toward the driveway.

Penelope took a picture of the sketch with her phone to text Joey, rolling her eyes when she saw the little circle spinning in frustration on her screen. She saved the text for the next time she visited the abandoned service station, what she was coming to think of as her mobile hotspot.

Chapter Thirty-Six

Thomas returned during lunch service with Nadia. She appeared to be fine, but more jumpy than usual. Penelope assumed it was the adrenaline from her accident. She'd become more aware of the after-effects of trauma in the past week or two, much more than she would have liked.

"I'm so glad you're okay," Penelope said as Nadia approached the dining tent.

"Just shaken up." Nadia hugged Penelope tightly, trembling slightly beneath her arms.

"Did you get a look at the driver? Anything about the car?" Penelope asked.

"She's been over all of this with the police," Thomas said. "She doesn't remember a thing." He left them alone and went into the tent, heading straight for the clean plates at the front of the food line.

"You didn't see anything?" Penelope asked.

"No," Nadia said. "It happened really fast, out of the blue. I was messing with the radio, looking at the map, and I saw a white flash. Next thing I was off the road, headed down the ravine. Penelope, it was so scary."

Penelope thought about Nadia's ever-present phone, but didn't ask her if she'd been texting while driving. Having a near-miss accident was punishment enough.

"Nadia," Penelope said, looking around them to see if anyone was close enough to hear. "I'm worried about you. What if all these things happening to you are connected?"

Nadia shook her head. "Why would someone want to hurt me?" Her voice hitched at the end, and she cleared her throat.

"What about that note to the police? Do you have any idea about it?" Penelope pressed her.

"I honestly have no clue," Nadia said. "Of course, everyone is watching me, all the time. I'm playing tennis on television half of the year. I have over a million followers on Twitter. I mean, it could be anyone."

"A million people?" Penelope murmured in disbelief. "Have you been threatened online?"

"Sure, there are trolls," Nadia said. "But they're just crazy people. I don't take it seriously. Everyone has haters."

Penelope thought about Arlena and how her absence from social media might be saving her a lot of uninvited negative opinions. "What kinds of things do people say?"

Nadia scoffed bitterly. "I've been called ugly, fat, a terrible tennis player. There's one troll who photoshops my head onto an ostrich and makes memes of me saying bird jokes. It's just what people do."

"I'm sorry, I didn't know that was happening," Penelope said.

"It's part of being a celebrity. I'm also a mentor. I coach kids in my off-season, and I get to do things like come on a film set with you. I'm a role model to young girls. An athlete. I've learned to take the good with the bad."

When they were teenagers, they were drawn together because they were both focused on having successful futures. They were good girls who didn't go out a lot, preferring to stay home and watch movies together. They bonded over being a bit nerdy while the cooler kids hung out at parties and the mall, sneaking drinks and cigarettes. "Wait,"

Penelope said, pulling her phone from her pocket and opening her text messages. "Do you know who this is?"

Nadia looked at the screen. Penelope kept her eyes on her old friend's face.

"Nope. Is it a sketch of Bradley Cooper in that movie with the aliens?"

"What? No," Penelope said. She clicked off the phone and put it back in her pocket.

"Where's Arlena?" Nadia asked, craning her neck to peer inside the tent.

"Upstairs in makeup," Penelope said. "They have to touch her up before they can pick back up again."

"Okay, well, I'm going to lie down for a while," Nadia said. "If I'm needed on the set, just send one of the P.A.s to wake me up."

"You're getting the movie lingo down pretty quickly," Penelope said.

"Yeah, I like this world. I'm going to take some acting classes. Jeremiah thinks I have potential, onscreen potential, he says. Then I'll have something to turn to when I retire, like Helen did with her artwork."

"Well, that's an interesting development. I didn't know acting was an interest of yours," Penelope said.

"We're all constantly growing," Nadia said. She turned and walked slowly up the back porch steps.

Chapter Thirty-Seven

Penelope returned to the boat house between lunch and dinner with a bus pan full of dishes. In the small kitchen, she loaded the dishwasher and filled the porcelain farmer's sink with warm, soapy water, gently laying a stack of dirty pans to soak. The team stayed up at the main house, cleaning the rest. Penelope had told them to take an hour to themselves before beginning on dinner. Jeremiah had promised a later night than usual, and she wanted to be sure they would all make it to the end.

Penelope sat in her favorite club chair and listened to the dishwasher drone in the kitchen behind her. Her eyes fell on the bookshelves, and she got up, wandering over to peruse the titles. She had always loved to read, even though these days, with her schedule, it might take her over a week to finish a book. Her shifts were sometimes sixteen hours long, which felt like all she did was work and sleep.

Penelope pulled a book from the shelf and flipped it open, recognizing the author's name as a famous New Englander. Thinking she'd already read that title, she crouched and pulled out another.

The small shiny button winked at her from behind. In her exhausted state earlier in the week, she thought she'd imagined seeing it there, but now fully rested, there it was again. Penelope stared at the tiny thing, a perfect brown circle, almost the same color as the bookshelf, with tiny pinholes covering the front. It looked a lot like a microphone, but not one that Penelope had ever seen before. A strange feeling passed over her then, a feeling of being exposed or watched. She flipped through all of the conversations she'd had in that room. They were all day-to-day ones, nothing she could point to as being something anyone would want to listen to.

Did she have some competitor who wanted to listen in on how she managed her staff? She laughed to herself at that possibility. No, this was either here before them, or meant for someone else.

Penelope went to the kitchen and pulled open a drawer, silverware clattering in the tray. Penelope opened the one next to it and found what she was looking for: a small silver spatula.

She went back to the bookcase and used it to pry the listening device from the bookcase. At first, it didn't give, then popped off with a shot, bouncing once on the shelf before landing on the carpet. Penelope coughed loudly as she picked it up, then stepped out onto the deck, holding the bug out with two fingers away from her body.

She set it down on the railing in the far corner and stared at it.

Not sure what to do next, Penelope left it and returned inside. She spent most of the next hour looking behind all of the books in the house and in all of the cabinets, too, making sure someone wasn't monitoring their every move.

Chapter Thirty-Eight

Penelope slipped behind the wheel of her Jeep and drove to her mobile hot spot in front of the abandoned service station. She had made a mental list of all the things she wanted to accomplish on the quick trip when she was connected to the rest of the world again. When she arrived, she parked quickly and turned off the engine.

First, she texted the sketch of her suspect to Joey with the words: "Can you find out who this is?" Next, she opened her Google app and typed in Nadia's full name. Fifteen pages of results appeared, and Penelope began scrolling through different articles and biography sites that had her listed. Not seeing anything out of the ordinary, she went back to the search bar and typed the word "arrest." Her heart skipped when the screen filled again, until she noticed the word "arrest" was lined out in fine print. She wasn't sure what she'd been hoping to find, possibly someone who had gotten into trouble and had a connection to Nadia Westin.

Penelope rubbed her eyes and leaned her head back against the seat, trying to think. "What is it about Nadia?" she said out loud to no one.

The phone buzzing in her lap made her jump. She answered quickly when she saw Joey's name.

"There's my love," Penelope said.

"I like that greeting," Joey said. "Who is this picture of?"

"That's what I want you to tell me," Penelope said. "I've been asking around, but I thought you might be able to run it through your computer."

"I can try," Joey said. "Who do we think this is?"

"I saw him up here and also at the bus stop across from Sonya's that day. I think. Maybe."

Joey's tone gained an edge. "This guy is following you?"

"Not me," Penelope said. "I think Nadia might have a stalker."

"Okay, I'll see what I can come up with."

"Also, is there a way to find out if Nadia's ever been associated with anyone who's a criminal? I keep feeling like someone is trying to get back at her for something."

"Yeah, I thought of that and did an initial search when the purse thing happened," Joey said. "I couldn't find anything linking her directly to any legal trouble, which I have to say is surprising. I thought all celebrity types fell prey to opportunists."

"Probably not everyone," Penelope said. "What else is happening at home? Any news?"

"We found the burning bag site," Joey said. "Well, Clarissa did."

"That's great!" Penelope said. "Finally, something. Where was it?"

"Wooded area behind the train station, a known transient and homeless camp. Problem is, there's an overwhelming amount of evidence back there, related and unrelated to our search."

"Her bag might still be out there, if you confirm the burnt one is a fake," Penelope said.

"Yeah, our guy in the lab says it's a knockoff," Joey said.

"Any idea how her purse and my money walked away from police custody?" Penelope asked.

Joey's voice became flat. "Clarissa thinks she's uncovered something in the evidence department. She's put together an undercover operation to roust out the culprit."

"Sounds like a good plan," Penelope said.

"Yeah, if you want to jam up other cops," Joey said.

"They're breaking the law, Joey," Penelope said.

Joey sighed. "I know, of course, you're right. It doesn't look good for us, though. A temporary detective showing us how corrupt we are."

"You aren't," Penelope said.

"Of course not," Joey said. "Okay, I have to put a call into your set, update Nadia about the handbag we found."

"Okay," Penelope said reluctantly. "Oh wait! I feel like I have to think of everything while I have you on the phone. What about the Letourneau connection between Sonya's and Lois's? Did you get my text?"

"I did," Joey said. "Yeah, there were Letourneaus at both incidents. Strange coincidence. So far, that's all it is, though. The crimes don't appear to be connected."

Penelope put her hand to her forehead and rubbed. "Okay. I'll call you soon."

"Bye, Penny Blue."

Penelope stared at her phone after he hung up, which had flipped back to the Google search screen. An article caught her eye, and she opened it, scanning through it quickly. Several tennis players the year before had been fined for using performance-enhancing substances. Penelope's eyes skipped through the names, a list of ten. Nadia's wasn't on it. She was mentioned elsewhere in the article as part of the tour that had been investigated, but she wasn't on the list of the ones who had been caught.

A text message popped up on her screen from Joey: "A name popped on your picture: Donald Matthews. Arrested for DUI six years ago, drunk and disorderly. Be careful if he shows up again."

Penelope swiped the text away and went back to the article she'd been reading on her phone. She scanned the list of names again, and her heart skipped when she came to the last one: Heather Matthews.

"Finally, maybe this is something," Penelope murmured. She Googled the girl's name and clicked on her Wikipedia listing: Heather Matthews, semi-professional tennis player. DOB: 3-14-1996. DOD: 6-12-2016.

Penelope stared at the date, then tapped the "Cause of Death" link. "Fatal Overdose."

Chapter Thirty-Nine

Penelope eyed Jeremiah during dinner, watching him talk with the crew as he ate. She spent a good amount of time watching Thomas, too. She had no idea who had put a listening device in the boathouse's living room, but her first suspicion fell on the owners. They had mentioned the boathouse and main house were often rented out to tourists when they weren't home. Maybe that was their way of keeping tabs on people while they were far away, making their movies. Penelope was relieved to find no other bugs in either the bedrooms or bathrooms, a small measure of relief. But she still felt their privacy had been violated, a feeling she wasn't used to.

Penelope didn't know much about spy devices, only what she'd seen in the movies, but this one didn't seem very sophisticated. She thought it might be short-range, not looking powerful enough to transmit a long way. But then again, she wasn't an expert.

When everyone was settled and eating dinner, Penelope went inside the main house and slipped up the stairs to the second floor. She tried the knob on the third door down, the room being used as the home office. Peeking in, she saw no one inside, so she gingerly stepped in and closed the door behind her. She didn't turn on the light, because the windows faced out onto the main lawn. If someone walked out from the tent and looked over at the house, they would see her. Luckily, a desk light had been left on, so she wasn't completely in the dark.

"Not good for the environment, leaving lights on like that," she mumbled.

Penelope had no idea what she was looking for. Some kind of radio, maybe, or a hidden panel with the label "spy network." She rolled her eyes and slid open a desk drawer, pausing first to look over her shoulder at the closed door.

Nothing electronic was in the desk. Just files and paperwork, what looked like rental agreements with summer visitors to the Truegood property. A file labeled Hefheiser caught her attention, and she pulled it out, flipping it open on the desk. She wasn't quite sure, but from what she read, the Truegood brothers owned majority shares in both Nate's market and the Hefheiser farm.

Penelope thought it was weird they hadn't mentioned any of that before. Especially since they were doing business with the farm and had sent her out to make a relationship with Nate on her own.

"Maybe it's something to do with the not wanting to mix their two business interests," she whispered to herself. "But still..."

She dug deeper in the file and found a copy of a letter of intent, signed by Nate Hefheiser, to sever ties with the Truegoods. It looked like an offer of a buyout, but Penelope couldn't tell if it had been executed or not. It was the top document in a larger stack, which Penelope quickly flipped through. A creak on the stairs outside quickened her heartbeat, and she tucked the papers back in the file. She returned them to the bottom file drawer, straightening them one last time before sliding the drawer closed.

The office door opened, and Penelope jumped up from her seat. The office chair spun lazily around a half circle as Jeremiah stuck his head in the door.

"Penelope," he said with a serene smile. "What are you doing in here?"

Penelope's stomach dropped, but her face remained calm. "I saw a light on in here, under the crack in the door. I was in the hallway, heading for the bathroom. Thought I'd turn it off, save some energy."

"Good thinking," Jeremiah said, eyeing the chair. "Dinner was amazing. It takes a skilled chef to cook duck perfectly for one hundred people."

Chapter Forty

Penelope lay in bed that night, turning over Hefheiser Farm, Nate, the Truegood brothers, the market, Nadia, Donald, and Heather Matthews, and the film production company in her mind. Why would Nate want to part ways with the obviously wealthy brothers? They were his cousins, he'd said. But they didn't appear particularly close, or friendly even. Farming wasn't an easy job, or always a profitable way of life. She remembered the calf born at the farm and the obvious pride Nate took in him, and the farm as a whole. If Nate had a strong financial backing through the Truegoods, why would he want to end it?

How well did Nadia know Heather Matthews? She must have known her well, if they'd been on tour together. Wouldn't she also recognize Heather's father? Penelope thought about Nadia's reaction to the picture on her phone. She had a tell when they were kids: she'd look down and away when she tried to pull off a lie. She'd kept her gaze straight at the screen, which made Penelope think she was telling the truth about not knowing Donald. If he was in trouble with the law, maybe he didn't hang around the tennis world as much Heather's mom, or another family member.

Tama breathed steadily from the other bed, quiet as always. Penelope closed her eyes and willed for sleep to come.

Half an hour later, Penelope was drifting off, but still partly awake, the puzzle in her mind keeping her from falling asleep completely. Tama silently lifted the blanket and slid out of bed, glancing quickly at Penelope before tip-toeing out of the bedroom.

Penelope pretended to sleep and listened to her movements on the other side of the door. She heard the French doors open, and Tama step onto the deck. Penelope let herself drift off, figuring Tama couldn't sleep and didn't want to disturb her. Maybe she was reading on the dock or meditating in the moonlight. Penelope's thoughts drifted and grew soft around the edges as she fell asleep.

Chapter Forty-One

The next morning, Penelope was surprised to see sunshine between the cracks in the blinds. She'd been up before dawn most mornings for meditation and silently thanked whoever forgot to rouse her that morning. Tama's bed was empty. Penelope wondered briefly what time it had been when she'd seen her leave the room. She was sure Tama hadn't missed meditation. It seemed like her favorite part of the day.

Lewis and Francis were out on the dock, drinking their coffee. Penelope poured a mug for herself and joined them, turning her face toward the rising sun and enjoying its warmth.

"It feels like we've been here for a month already," Lewis said. He had his bare foot up on the railing and rocked himself in his chair. "When's the weekend coming?"

Penelope knew "weekend" could mean any two days that they had off together, no matter which days they fell during the week. Sometimes their weekend was Tuesday and Wednesday, if production decided to work through the traditional weekends.

"I don't know," Penelope said. "It feels like they're moving through the script quickly, though. Not a lot of retakes so far."

"What's this thing?" Francis said, bouncing the brown, fake wood bug in his palm.

"Some kind of speaker," Penelope said. She had popped the back off the day before and removed the little round battery. It was in her suitcase now, in case someone came looking for it.

They talked about the menu for the day and went back inside a few minutes later to get dressed and head to the house.

* * *

"Where's Tama?" Penelope asked as they got to the kitchen. Francis began making a pot of coffee, and Lewis pulled out a large flat of eggs. They'd decided to do an omelet station that morning for the crew up early, preparing for the day's shoot.

"He can't do this!" a man yelled from the front hallway.

Penelope's team froze and looked toward the door.

"Calm down," Thomas said.

Penelope stepped out into the hallway to see what was happening. She was surprised to see Nate standing there, his face red and his body taut, standing toe to toe with Thomas in the front foyer.

"I've backed down before, but I'm not going to be weak this time," Nate yelled. A few of the crew stood on the stairway, watching the altercation. "You're not going to get away with this again."

"Nathaniel, take it easy," Thomas said. "Jeremiah can do what he likes as long as the bank agrees."

Nate's face turned a darker shade of red. "Your promises once again mean nothing!" he yelled. He swiped his hand at the wall and knocked a framed photo onto the ground, shattering the glass.

Penelope took a step back, the shock of seeing the normally kind Nate so angry was jarring.

"Nathaniel," Thomas said again, trying to calm Nate down.

"It's Nate," he spat. "I'm not a child anymore. Not like how you and that brother of yours act, playing around up here with your feelings, putting on make-believe out in LA like little boys. Some of us actually work for a living."

"No one works harder than you, Nathan…Nate," Thomas agreed. "That's why we've always helped you. We're family."

"Helped me?" Nate asked sarcastically. "That's a good one. You waited until the bank was just about to foreclose on the family farm. Our family farm, until my father had a heart attack from the stress and died right there in the barn. He begged your father, you, and your brother to help, and what do you do? You let us go to auction, then swoop in."

"We did it to save the farm," Thomas said, raising his palms.

"No, you bought the farm out from under us, at bottom dollar. And now my family works for yours, following all your crazy rules. Don't use this pesticide, don't ship to customers outside a twenty-mile radius, or to anyone who doesn't live up to your crazy environmental standards. You don't know the first thing about running a farm. You work in make-believe."

"Nate, let's sit down and discuss this over breakfast," Thomas motioned to Penelope, standing at the end of the hall. Her eyes fell to the shattered glass on the floor, a black and white family photo under the shards.

Nate's eyes bored into Penelope's, and his expression hardened. He turned to go without another word, stomping down the back steps to his truck. He peeled down the driveway, a dusty cloud from the gravel trailing behind him.

* * *

"What happened?" Penelope asked Thomas in the foyer after the dust had cleared and everyone had gone back to their tasks.

"I don't know. This time," Thomas said. "I do know he and Jeremiah have always gone at it, ever since we were kids."

"But what happened today to make him flip out like that? Was it something we did?"

"Why would you say that?" Thomas asked.

"Well, honestly, I had no idea there was a family connection with you guys until I found out for myself. Weird no one mentioned it. And I obviously didn't know there was hostility, but I should have figured it out, I guess," Penelope said. She remembered the paperwork she had found upstairs in the house and decided the family tension had gone back a ways. "What set Nate off today?"

Thomas put his hands on his hips and considered for a moment. "Nathaniel's grandfather owned a service station out on the main road. It's been out of business going on ten years now, but he's held onto it, hoping to bring it back one day," Thomas said.

"I think I know which one you mean," Penelope said. He motioned for her to take a seat on the bench swing next to him.

"Jeremiah just put an offer in to buy it," Thomas said.

"Well, that's a good thing, right?" Penelope said.

"Not according to Nathaniel," Thomas said. "To him, that means my side of the family now owns everything his side of the family once did. Plus, Jeremiah wants to tear the station down and build a high-end bistro, a tourist spot for the summer people and the skiers. The same rich ones who rent out this whole place for a month without thinking twice about the cost. His idea is to get a celebrity chef to move to Micklesburg, make it a destination spot."

"Well, Nate can refuse the deal, right?" Penelope said.

"Not if Jeremiah forces the issue, decides to let the farm go if he doesn't get his way," Thomas said, shaking his head. "Our ownership and investment keep it going. Without us, Nate and the farm would go under in a year, maybe sooner."

"So, Nate's livelihood is dependent on the two of you. He's got no choice then, really," Penelope said. "I mean, I guess he could stop living the only life he's ever known. Stop working on the farm that has been in his family for hundreds of years."

Thomas looked at her sheepishly.

"Basically, Nate's in a position where he has to sell the station or risk losing the farm," Penelope said evenly.

One of the production SUVs turned into the driveway. Jeremiah was at the wheel, and Penelope was surprised to see Tama in the passenger seat. He parked the car, and they stepped out, Tama carrying a mesh produce bag.

Tama shot her a glance as they climbed the porch steps. Penelope gazed at her from the swing.

"Jeremiah, let's talk inside," Thomas said, standing up and motioning him through the front door.

"Where were you?" Penelope asked after the brothers had gone inside. Tama had her chef coat slung over one arm, and was wearing jeans and a t-shirt with their culinary school logo on the front.

"I went with Jeremiah into town after meditation. He had something to do at the courthouse that took longer than expected. I wanted to get some lemons for you. I saw your notes in the kitchen about making a curd."

Penelope softened a bit but kept her eyes steady.

"I'm sorry I'm late," Tama said. She looked Penelope in the eye, her expression serene.

Penelope finally said, "I was a little worried when I couldn't find you. Next time, leave a note so I know you're okay."

"I didn't know I was going to be late, or I would have," Tama said.

"A note, Tama," Penelope insisted. "It takes two seconds."

Tama nodded. "Yes, Chef."

"The guys are in the tent. Go help get breakfast ready," Penelope said. "It already feels like a very long day around here."

Chapter Forty-Two

Lunch and dinner were going to be served up at the courts again that day. They had a smaller crowd to feed, but a number of extras had been hired to add background to an argument scene between Arlena and her costar, the guy playing Phil Neer.

Penelope watched the young man play opposite Arlena. He had such fine features and a delicate nose, but he was convincing when he played angry. As was Arlena, although for her, it wasn't quite as much of a stretch for Penelope to imagine. She and Arlena had never been in a real argument, but they'd lived together long enough for Penelope to witness many emotions and vice versa. She thought about the last night she'd spent with Joey, how he'd talked about living together. She knew that would be completely different than living with just a friend, but followed the logical train of thought that it would deepen their relationship and change it in many ways. Penelope sighed, thinking she hadn't had a chance to call him the past day, and she missed hearing his voice. But she also secretly welcomed this brief time apart. It gave her time to think about her decision, without the pull of him near her, without her emotions taking over and making decisions for her.

Jeremiah wrapped the scene, and her team worked through lunch. She was proud of them. This wasn't the easiest set to manage. The easiest was a sound stage in a big studio, if she told the truth. All of this running up and down the mountain added a new dimension to their jobs, and she was proud of how they all rolled with the flow.

"I'll run the stuff back down to the house today," Penelope said. "Lewis, you come and help me. You two," she nodded at Tama and Francis, "start prepping dinner."

Nadia and Arlena sat in their usual place, eating salads together again. Penelope slipped out without talking to anyone, anxious to get back to the house, then take a moment to call Joey.

* * *

Penelope pulled into the familiar parking lot of what she now knew was Nate's gas station. Or soon to be not his gas station. It still looked sad, no matter who owned it. She wondered what Nate's parents had been like when they were young and building a life together here. Before things changed for them.

She pulled her phone from the glove box and called Joey, a smile spreading on her face at the anticipation of hearing his voice.

"You aren't going to believe it," Joey said first.

"Hello to you, too," Penelope said.

"We caught the boys," Joey said. "The ones who attacked Sonya's cafe."

"Oh wow," Penelope said. "When?"

"Early this morning," Joey said. He was keeping his voice down, but Penelope could hear the excitement in his voice. "They were living in a house with half a dozen other guys, all Russian nationals, most of them here illegally."

"That's so great, Joey," Penelope said. "What a relief to have justice for Sonya's family."

"It was your tip that led us to them," Joey said. "The team jersey and jackets aren't sold anymore, but you can get them online. We tracked a box of them to a memorabilia store two towns over. The shop owner gave us a name and location."

"That was good of him," Penelope said.

"Well, he didn't want to, but he had some outstanding warrants of his own, tax problems, so he decided cooperating with us was better than the alternative," Joey said.

"Well, I'm glad he did the right thing, however it happened."

A pickup truck passed by, and Penelope glanced over as it slowed near the gas station's parking lot. Traffic was so infrequent on this road, she thought it might be one of the only vehicles she'd seen out here. The truck came almost to a stop as the driver tapped the brakes. The back window was too dark to see through. The tags were an unfamiliar light blue, with the words "Live Free or Die" blazed across the top. The numbers and the rest of the plate were obscured by mud splatter that went up both sides of the truck.

"Live Free or Die," Penelope said softly.

"They also admitted they robbed the coffee shop, too," Joey continued.

"They did?" Penelope asked. The pickup truck came to a stop, and the driver revved the engine. Penelope sat up straighter in her seat.

"Yeah, we were able to connect fingerprints to both crime scenes," Joey said.

The pickup truck began rolling forward again, and Penelope eased back in her seat.

"Can you text me pictures of the boys?" Penelope asked. "I'll testify if I need to, of course. Anything to help Sonya and Mirabelle."

"Sure," Joey said. "We've confirmed IDs with a couple of the witnesses. Another from you would make our case that much stronger."

"What does 'Live Free or Die' mean on a license plate?" Penelope asked.

"That's the New Hampshire state motto," Joey said. "I thought you were in Vermont."

"I am," Penelope said. "But that's close by, right?"

"Couple of hours away, depending on where you are," Joey said.

Her phone pinged, and she pulled it away from her ear. She opened the text message and the picture Joey had sent. "The first one is the one who held the door. With the dark hair," Penelope said. She nodded when she opened the second photo. "And the light-haired kid is the one who had the stick. Nadia will be so relieved."

Joey blew out a sigh when a phone started ringing in the background. "Penny, I have to take this call. Call me back soon, okay?"

"Love you," Penelope said, not wanting to hang up.

"Love you too," Joey said.

Chapter Forty-Three

The crew worked late into the night, and Jeremiah called for a late dinner down at the house. He and Thomas decided to give everyone the following day off to rest and reflect on the first few days of filming and wanted to open a few bottles from his cellar to celebrate.

Penelope bit her tongue when she heard his plans after she and Lewis had already driven most of the entrees up the mountain to meet them at the courts. But she kept her cool, and her team followed her lead.

"At least we hadn't unpacked anything," Penelope said. "Let's get the salad bar wrapped up and moved."

They worked quickly in clearing down the salad bar and steam tables in the tent and re-packing their truck. Just as they were shrink-wrapping their final tower of food, Jeremiah appeared in the parking area, arms crossed over his chest.

"That's a lot of plastic," he remarked as they finished loading the last cart up the ramp.

"We reuse it as much as we can," Penelope said truthfully.

"Okay, just keep in mind every inch of plastic that people use kills two fish in the ocean," Jeremiah said as he began to walk away.

"That sounds made up," Francis murmured. Lewis snickered under his breath. Tama stayed characteristically quiet, but her usual smile was replaced with an expression of worry.

"You guys get back to the lake house and set up," Penelope said. "I'll catch a ride down." She followed Jeremiah across the parking lot and reached up, putting a hand on his shoulder. He turned around and smiled at her, as if he hadn't seen her in a very long time.

"Penelope, thanks for working hard. I know you can't be perfect with the plastic, but I appreciate your efforts." Jeremiah beamed down on her.

Penelope had been geared up to argue with him, but his encouraging praise made her soften her stance.

"What is it?" Jeremiah asked as she gathered herself.

"Nate was by the house this morning," Penelope said. "He was really angry."

"Ah, Cousin Nathaniel," Jeremiah said, crossing his arms again. "Thomas told me. I'm sorry he caused a scene."

"It's not that," Penelope said. "Is there any way to meet him halfway? He seems like such a nice, decent man. I get the feeling he feels like an employee of yours, not an equal member of the family."

Jeremiah smiled at her and sharpened his gaze. "We're all equal members of a family. Humankind."

"But you own most of everything he's involved in," Penelope insisted.

"Why are you so concerned about him?" Jeremiah asked.

"Well…" Penelope thought on her feet. "You've shown me through your beliefs, the meditation, and your causes to save the planet that you're a kind man. Also, that we can't own the earth."

Jeremiah laughed quickly. "Better we own it than the bank, right? Should we have watched Nathaniel's family farm get taken out from under him?"

"No, but…" Penelope began.

"It's kind of you," Jeremiah said, "to worry about things the way you do. But this isn't something to put your energy behind. Keeping our assets in the family is best, and Thomas and I are in a position to do that."

"Well, in order to keep the peace in the family, maybe you could loosen some of your rules, or gift him the service station," Penelope suggested.

"And watch him mortgage it away to immoral bankers again?" Jeremiah shook his head. "Penelope, you lovely woman, some people are no good at managing things. Some people are. We have no issue here. Let's focus on the things we're good at. Speaking of which, shouldn't you be making dinner for our guests?"

Penelope's face flushed, and Jeremiah put a hand on her cheek. "Such heat from you. You have a fiery spirit, Penelope. That's what carries you forward, makes you a beacon of light people are bound to follow. Remember that when you're showing people the way. Be careful you're not leading them into danger." Penelope eased away from his touch, putting more space between them. Jeremiah often became too close, both to her and others on the set. She chalked it up to his general personality, his intense connections he attempted to make with everyone around him.

Jeremiah turned and walked away, waving to a cluster of crew members hovering near the sound truck.

"I never know what he's saying," Penelope mumbled to herself. "But I always know what he means." She touched her fingers to the place on her cheek where his hand had been and thought about Tama stepping from his car earlier that day.

Chapter Forty-Four

Penelope and her crew found themselves hosting a week's end wrap-up party back at the tent in the front yard of the lake house. Jeremiah put a call out to all of the extras they'd had that week to join them if they could. Penelope kept a running tally in her head of what they had prepared and what they had on hand they could quickly pull together to feed the growing crowd.

Thomas hefted two cases of liquor bottles in his long arms through the flaps of the tent and placed them on one of the side tables. Tama opened the boxes and started setting up the bar with a variety of vodka, gin, and rum bottles. "I'll cut some fruit," she said to herself, arranging the bottles just so.

Arlena entered along with Nadia; they had both changed into jeans and button-down shirts. Penelope wondered if they consulted with each other on what to wear before coming to the party.

"Hey guys," Penelope said. "Help yourself to some dinner. And a cocktail."

Penelope's crew did a great job of hosting the impromptu celebration, dishing out entrees, and pouring drinks. The tent was almost full, and Penelope figured there were a hundred and twenty people inside, including everyone who had anything to do with the film so far.

"Thanks," Arlena said as they headed to the makeshift bar.

"Cosmopolitan?" a man's voice tickled Penelope's ear. She turned around quickly to see Jeremiah standing behind her, his long hair loose around his shoulders. He'd changed into a fitted black t-shirt and jeans, his handsome face smiling in the glowing lanterns hanging around the tent.

"I'm working," Penelope said.

"I insist," Jeremiah said. "And your team, too. You four are a big part of our success this week. Join us in celebrating with a drink or two."

Penelope eyed the bar and admitted she'd love a good martini. "Okay, it's been quite a week, so we will. Thanks, Jeremiah."

Jeremiah smiled and wandered away, pausing to chat with Tama. Penelope watched them for a moment before waving Francis over.

"Have a drink if you want," she said.

The crowd noise began to rise, and Penelope stood in one corner, watching the guests and keeping an eye on the steam tables. When it appeared everyone had stopped helping themselves, she motioned for her team to begin breaking everything down.

"Then you can hang out however long you like," she told them. "We're off tomorrow."

Lewis pulled a fist down in the air and hissed, "yes."

"Don't go crazy," Penelope warned, laughing at him. "No hangovers, yes?"

"Of course not, Boss," Francis said, suppressing a grin. "How much trouble can you possibly get into around here anyway?"

Penelope wandered away to where Arlena was talking and laughing with the actor who was playing her onscreen opponent. He grinned at something she said, and they both broke out laughing.

"You guys look like you're having fun. Unlike your characters, who are always arguing," Penelope said.

"It's hard to argue with Arlena off-screen," he said. He stood up from the table. "I need a refill. Anyone else?"

They both shook their heads, and he headed toward the bar.

"Where's Nadia?" Penelope asked. "You guys are joined at the hip these days." Penelope felt a twinge of possessiveness toward Arlena, but quickly put it aside, realizing it was immature.

"She wandered off a while ago," Arlena said. "She takes a lot of selfies. I mean *a lot*," Arlena said, laughing.

"Yeah, I think she's known for them," Penelope said.

"Having fun?" Arlena asked, scanning the crowd.

"Sure," Penelope said. She sat down next to Arlena and looked around with her. She hadn't seen the bearded man at the party all night. Again, she wondered if she'd imagined the whole thing.

A scream from outside the tent filled the night, and a wave of silence passed over the noisy crowd. Another scream propelled Penelope from her seat, and out of the nearest flap, Arlena and several others following her.

Tama stood at the edge of the front porch, her hands covered in blood. Nadia lay at her feet, face down in the grass, red stains on her collar.

"Call an ambulance," Penelope yelled. She ran to Nadia and bent down, feeling her neck for a pulse.

Thomas came out of the house, hugging another case of liquor in his arms. "What happened?"

"I don't know, but she needs help," Penelope said.

Thomas set the box on the porch and hurried back inside.

"Is she dead?" Tama cried. She held her hands away from her as Nadia's blood dripped from her fingers.

"She has a pulse," Penelope said.

Jeremiah came down the porch steps and pushed through the crowd of onlookers that had gathered around Nadia. He knelt down on the opposite side of Penelope. He looked at Nadia in disbelief for a moment, then went to roll her over.

"No!" Penelope said. "She's got a head injury. I don't think we should move her."

Jeremiah looked afraid, the first time Penelope had seen that expression on his face. He looked up at Tama's face and then her hands. "Why? She and you both are the world to me. I love you both equally. You're my spiritual partners on this project."

"What?" Tama cried. "I didn't do anything to her. I found Nadia this way. I was trying to help her."

Penelope watched his expression move from relief to realization as his eyes found hers. "Who then? Who would hurt such a beautiful person?"

A siren sounded far off in the distance.

"How are they here so quickly?" Penelope asked.

"Volunteer firemen and paramedics are in every community for emergencies. They have satellite offices. They'll have to take her to Burlington if she's critical," Jeremiah said, seeming to return to reality at the sound.

Nadia began to moan, and Penelope squeezed her hand lightly. "We're here, Nadia. Help is coming."

Penelope saw a tear slip down her old friend's cheek, and she felt a wave of her own tears threatening.

The ambulance bounced up the driveway, red lights flashing brightly against the white tent. Two older men jumped out and ran to them, one of them doubling back to grab a long board when they saw Nadia in the grass. Jeremiah urged the crowd to stand back to give them room to work.

Penelope stepped back also, but she kept her eyes on Nadia's face the whole time. They were open now, which was encouraging, but she didn't seem to be able to focus on anything. Blood seeped from a gash on her head, and her arm sat at an odd angle.

"Arm's broken in at least two places," one of the emergency workers said as he gingerly cut through the sleeve of her shirt.

Nadia seemed to rouse at that, and the other EMT urged her to quiet down. She began to cry in earnest as they fitted her with a neck brace and hoisted her onto the longboard, keeping her broken arm stable.

"This is awful," Penelope said as they carried her to the ambulance. She felt sick to her stomach and clutched it as she doubled over.

Tama sat on the porch steps, staring at the blood on her hands. Penelope sat next to her, stunned, and watched the ambulance speed away.

"We have to talk," Penelope said quietly.

Tama nodded. "I know."

Chapter Forty-Five

"It's got to be one of us, right?" Francis asked. The party had broken up, and Penelope and her team were back at the boat house. "Where are the police around here?"

"There's a constable coming from the neighboring town, I heard," Lewis said.

Tama stared at her hands, which were folded together in her lap.

"What's a constable?" Lewis asked. "Don't they have those in England?"

"Guys," Penelope said, "did anyone see anything? We are in a good position to notice everyone on a set. We see all the faces twice a day, coming through the food line. Did anyone look unfamiliar? Stand out to you in any way?"

They both shook their heads. Lewis sighed and stood up. "Who else wants a beer?"

Francis raised his hand, and Penelope shook her head no. Tama continued to stare downward.

"Francis, give us a minute, will you?" Penelope asked softly.

Francis nodded and followed Lewis inside, closing the door behind them.

"What happened, Tama?" Penelope asked, touching her hand.

Tama jerked out of her daze and pulled her hand away, then rubbed it quickly on her jeans. "I was heading up to the house to get more wine glasses. I heard a cracking noise, a sick-sounding thud, and a muffled cry of pain. It was awful, like an animal being killed." Tama shivered. "I heard someone run off, and I went to see if there was a dead animal or an injured one, so close to the house…then I, I…"

She began to breathe heavily, and a sob came from her throat.

Penelope thought back to the tent and the dozens of unused glasses on the wine table.

"You were going inside to meet Jeremiah, weren't you?" Penelope asked gently.

Tama's face crumpled in sorrow, and fresh sobs erupted from the girl. Penelope glanced at the French doors and squeezed her hand tighter.

"I'm sorry," Tama choked.

"It's okay," Penelope soothed. "I'm not mad at you."

"You're not?" Tama asked, brightening through her storm of tears.

"Well, you were supposed to be working," Penelope said. "But you're a grown woman. A young woman, but you're old enough to make your own choices. I've noticed how much attention Jeremiah pays to you." And to others, Penelope refrained from saying.

Tama looked relieved, and her chest stopped heaving as sharply. "I was sure you'd be really angry."

"Tama," Penelope said, "you're a smart girl with a bright future. I see your potential. Clearly, Jeremiah does, too."

"Yeah," Tama said weakly. "He wants me to stay here and work as a chef at a new restaurant he's opening."

"That's huge for someone your age," Penelope said. "I don't know that I appreciate him poaching one of my people, but I understand why he would."

Tama hugged Penelope suddenly, hanging on tightly to her neck. "I'm so confused," she whispered wetly in Penelope's ear.

Penelope was taken aback by Tama's sudden emotion. She was

normally so sedate, verging on shy. This was a new side to her altogether. She rubbed her young chef's back and said, "Listen to your gut. You'll know what the right choice is, I promise."

Tama eased back onto the deck chair and wiped mascara from beneath her eyes.

"One thing," Penelope said. "And I don't want to upset you, but what did Jeremiah mean when he said you and Nadia were both the world to him?"

Tama laughed, her serene smile reappearing on her face. "It's a meditation thing. He said we were his two strongest orbs right now, that we could bring him to the meditative state faster than anyone."

"Oh, okay," Penelope said. She watched Tama as she settled back in the chair and thought maybe she didn't have the whole story when it came to Jeremiah Truegood. Penelope wasn't sure if he was attempting to throw the widest net possible, gathering potential companions to his side, or if he was just on a different plane altogether when it came to attraction and love.

Chapter Forty-Six

The next morning, Penelope got up early and slipped out of the boat house without waking Tama or the guys in the adjoining bedroom. She made her way around the house quietly. She doubted Jeremiah would host a meditation circle right next to where one of his favorite meditation partners had been attacked, but she also wasn't sure how Jeremiah thought about things either. Better to be safe than sorry.

The lawn was clear, the dining tent abandoned. Chairs and tables were in disarray. Some of the chairs toppled over on their backs. On a normal night, she and her crew would have set everything perfectly to greet the morning crowds. Considering what had happened and the fact that they had the day off, Penelope let them go home without straightening up.

Penelope glanced up at the house and saw no movement. She walked carefully through the damp grass to the spot where Nadia had been attacked. Her stomach turned slightly when she saw a dark patch of blood and pictured Nadia's arm bent in the wrong place. She was about to turn and go when something shiny caught her eye from under the bushes. Bending down and parting two branches, Penelope spotted Nadia's phone, the sparkly purple jeweled case reflecting the soft morning sun.

Penelope looked at it for a moment, then reached to grab it, being careful to pick it up at the edges with her fingertips. Slipping it in her sweater pocket, she went up the porch steps and pulled on the front door handle, which was locked. Penelope fished around in her other pocket for her set of keys and let herself into the main house.

Penelope put a pot of coffee on in the main kitchen and sat down at the table, waiting for it to brew. She gingerly removed the phone from her pocket and placed it on the table in front of her, pausing for a moment, then swiping it open.

"No passcode," Penelope mumbled. The coffee gurgled behind her as she navigated to Nadia's photos. She tapped it and let out a low whistle. "Eight thousand photos?" She sighed and opened the first one. It was a picture of her and Arlena in the tent the night before at the party. There were eight more just like it, taken one after the other. That seemed to be a pattern. The next several pictures were of the food, then some of her staff, and at least twenty crowd pictures.

The coffee pot beeped, and Penelope got up to pour a cup. She sat back down and went through the crowd pictures more closely, enlarging them with her fingers here and there to get a closer look at faces. She didn't know what she was looking for, but hoped to catch a glance of the man from the bus stop.

He didn't show up in any of them, so Penelope went further back in time, swiping through the last few days of Nadia's life. There were a hundred or so of Arlena playing tennis on the court and several crowd shots of the stands.

Penelope took a sip of coffee and froze when she saw his face. Her finger hovered over the glass as the man with the stained lip stared up at her from the table, a look of menace on his face. It wasn't from the first day at the courts, from what she could tell. It was from the day before, when they started out there, then had to move everything back to the main house for the party.

"Good morning," Jeremiah said from the doorway. He had on cargo shorts and was shirtless, his arms crossed at his chest as he leaned in the doorway.

Penelope mumbled a greeting and clicked the phone closed.

"I just called the medical center," Jeremiah said quietly. "They've transported Nadia to Burlington to have surgery on her arm. She was hit on the head, has a concussion. But the arm is the big thing."

"How did it happen?" Penelope asked. "Can the doctors tell anything?"

Jeremiah looked out the kitchen window toward the lake, his expression stricken. "They think someone stomped on it. There were shoe marks on her skin."

Penelope put a hand over her eyes and concentrated on breathing. The edges of her vision began to fuzz over, but she brought herself back around, focusing on his voice and the scent of coffee.

She swiped open the phone and said, "Who is this?"

Jeremiah stood next to her chair and looked down at the photo of the man on the screen. "I'm not sure."

"If you know who he is, you better tell me. Or the police," Penelope said in a threatening tone.

"I've never seen him before," he said firmly. He was so close Penelope could smell the scent of soap on his skin. She inched away from him.

"What's going on with you and Nadia?" Penelope asked.

Jeremiah went to the coffee maker and poured himself a mug. "We're connected. Spiritually."

"Is that what you call it?" Penelope scoffed.

"I see you doubting me," Jeremiah said. "That's your right."

Penelope bit her tongue, then reconsidered and said, "You're in a position of power. Over women and men. You should be careful where and how you wield it." With that, she stood up and left through the back door, snatching the phone from the table and tucking it in her pocket.

Chapter Forty-Seven

Penelope pulled her Jeep into the parking lot of the Micklesburg Market. The sun was warm that morning, and she welcomed the warmth on her shoulders.

"Good morning, Cheri," Penelope said as she walked through the door.

Cheri was behind the counter in her usual spot, leafing through another magazine.

"Penelope," Cheri said, nodding. "Nice to see you again."

"I have something to show you," Penelope said, reaching into her sweater pocket. She opened the photo app and enlarged the face of the man with the stained lip. "You said you saw him before, right?"

"Yeah," Cheri said, nodding. "First Tuesday last month."

"How do you know it was that exact day?" Penelope asked.

"That's when *THEM* magazine comes out. I always read the new copies when they come in, keep up with the news."

Penelope closed her eyes for a second, then opened them and said. "You saw him in a magazine? I thought you meant you saw him here."

"I never said that," Cheri said defensively.

"Okay," Penelope said. "My mistake." She sighed. "You wouldn't still have a copy of that one, would you?"

Cheri smiled, which looked unusual on her normally flat, expressionless face. "I do."

Cheri crouched down and opened a sliding door beneath the counter. After rifling through a stack, she stood up, a dog-eared magazine in her hand. "Page 29."

"You remember the page?" Penelope asked incredulously.

Cheri shrugged. "I remember stuff like that."

Penelope turned to the page she indicated, halfway thinking she would be wrong, and found herself staring at a photo of the man with the stained lip. Donald Matthews.

"Oh my…" Penelope said. "…God," she finished as she read the article.

"You think he's up here? In Micklesburg?" Cheri said, craning her neck to see the article.

"I know he is. I'm afraid I know why, too," Penelope said. "Some kind of obsession with my friend, or he blames her for what happened to his daughter."

"What happened to his daughter?" Cheri asked.

"She died."

Cheri looked at her placidly, although Penelope saw a touch of sadness in her eyes. "Is Nate here?"

"In the office," Cheri said.

Nate opened the door after Penelope knocked twice. He looked at her sheepishly, his hands tucked into the front pocket of his jeans.

"I'm sorry about the other morning," Nate said. "I'm embarrassed you saw me acting that way."

"Nate, I get it," Penelope said. "No need to apologize. I have something to tell you. It's important. But first, can I borrow your phone?"

Chapter Forty-Eight

Penelope sped down the two-lane road toward the medical center at the edge of Micklesburg. The trees blotted out the sun in spots as she passed in and out of shadow, and Penelope thought about the picture she'd seen. Finally, she had a name to put to the face. The face she'd been seeing over and over again. Donald Matthews.

Penelope pulled into the medical center and walked to the front desk. A tired-looking woman in nurse scrubs buzzed her through the door and into the back, where a nurse's desk anchored the back wall, and three rooms lined the walls on either side.

Nadia dozed in a hospital bed, her head and one eye covered in bandages. Her arm was in a cast and was suspended slightly above her chest. Penelope approached her quietly, studying the face of the girl she'd known so long ago. The one who had become famous, the fierce competitor.

Nadia stirred when she got to the edge of her bed.

"Penelope," Nadia whispered. Her voice was thick and slow.

"How are you?" Penelope asked. It seemed a silly question at the moment, but she didn't know how else to ask.

"Awful," Nadia said, closing her eye.

"They're moving you soon," Penelope said. "Donald won't be able to hurt you again. I've called the police. They know to keep you safe."

"Donald?" Nadia croaked, then shook her head once. Gooseflesh broke out on her arms. "Why?"

"What were you doing in New Hampshire the other day?" Penelope asked gently. "You told us you were going to Burlington, but I checked your phone after they took you away. You searched an address in New Hampshire in the other direction."

A tear slipped down Nadia's cheek. "I offered them money. Heather's family blames me for what happened, for everything."

"They blame you for their daughter's death?" Penelope asked.

Nadia nodded slowly, pain causing her to grimace.

"Heather Matthews overdosed," Penelope said. "Why do her parents think it's your fault?"

Nadia fell silent for a moment, and Penelope thought she'd fallen asleep. She sat down in the chair next to the bed and waited.

"I was the senior player on the women's tennis team," Nadia said groggily. "We competed separately, but we trained together, traveled as a unit. Lived together. I introduced Heather to my personal trainer."

"Then what happened?" Penelope asked.

"Heather was falling behind," Nadia said, opening her eyes and looking at Penelope again. "She thought drugs were the answer. My trainer always said they were herbal, that they wouldn't show up on any tests. I know how to trick the tests. I told Heather how to also, but she didn't listen."

"The article I read said she was ejected from the team," Penelope said. "And later overdosed on prescription drugs. Why do you have to beat the drug tests? Are you taking something you shouldn't?"

Nadia's voice hardened. "You don't know what it's like in my world. Being an athlete, competing for a living. How would you feel if your job, your livelihood, was on the line every day? You have a bad day, a bad match, and your career is over. You...you cook a bad meal, and you still have a job the next day."

"Not quite the same," Penelope hedged.

"You don't have to strain yourself physically day in and day out," Nadia continued.

Penelope let her talk, unconvinced cheating was the only path to success for athletes. Who was she to judge someone else? She glanced at Nadia's broken arm and felt she'd been judged enough lately.

"I saw Heather's father at the tennis courts," Nadia said. "He's been furious with me, has left me threatening messages, driven by my house."

"He followed you all the way to Vermont," Penelope said.

Nadia winced and closed her eye again. This time, she did fall asleep, her breaths falling into a regular rhythm.

Penelope left the room quietly and stepped into the hallway. Three nurses sat at the main desk in blue scrubs, two of them staring at monitors and one talking quietly on the phone. She took a few steps away from Nadia's room and pulled out her phone.

"No cell phones in here," one of the nurses called quietly to her.

Penelope nodded and pushed the door into the lobby. A doctor passed her on the way, wearing the same powder blue scrubs as the others and a white jacket. He brushed Penelope's shoulder as she scrolled through the messages on her phone, and she looked over her shoulder at him as he hurried past. He ducked his head as he studied a chart in his hand, his sooty black hair dampening his collar.

Penelope put her phone to her ear and called Joey. As she listened to the rings, she looked back through the double windows on the doors and saw the man pause at the nurses' desk, then proceed to Nadia's room. Penelope went to the parking lot after glancing at the waiting room attendant.

"There she is," Joey said.

"A lot has happened since we spoke," Penelope said. "We had an incident on the set and…"

"Penelope?" Joey asked after her pause went on a bit long.

At the edge of the parking area, Penelope spotted a familiar pickup truck. The mud was gone, but she remembered the license plate numbers. And the big words that read "Live Free or Die."

"I have to call you back," Penelope said. She walked toward the truck and looked in the window. The floor was littered with paper, a map book of Vermont, and fast-food wrappers. On the floor of the passenger seat was a crumpled hair dye box with a man staring up at her with dark black hair.

Penelope remembered the sooty tint of the doctor's hair, and her legs went numb. She turned and bolted back inside the medical center.

"Call the police," Penelope shouted at the waiting room attendant. Her eyes widened, and she stared uncomprehending. "Now!" The woman picked up her phone with shaking hands and dialed.

Penelope pushed back through to the nurses' area and through Nadia's door. The nurses stared after her, unmoving, and then one of them sprung into action, coming out from behind the large desk.

"She's in with the doctor," the nurse called.

"I don't think so," Penelope said over her shoulder.

When she entered the room, she saw a sleeping Nadia and the "doctor" sitting in the chair next to the bed, staring at her.

"What are you doing, Mr. Matthews?" Penelope asked. Her heart was pounding, but she kept her voice level.

He looked up at her, blonde roots under his shiny black hair. The wine stain quivered on his lower lip. Nadia woke at the sound of her voice and looked startled as the man dressed as a doctor stood up and hovered over her.

"She had everything going for her," he said in an oddly calm voice. "We sacrificed everything we had. Lessons, pro consults, up before dawn, driving to practices and matches for years. Then you come along, and now…"

He reached over Nadia and gently put his hands around her neck.

CHAPTER FORTY-EIGHT

"Stand back," Penelope said.

The nurse came into the room and stood behind Penelope. "Oh!" she yelled.

Mr. Matthews panicked at that and began to squeeze. Nadia choked out, "Help."

Penelope closed the space between them and threw her arm around the man's neck, pulling as hard as she could in a headlock. Donald released Nadia's neck and whipped around, trying to throw Penelope off his back.

"Stay out of this," he sputtered. "It wasn't your little girl."

Penelope pressed harder as Don backed her into the wall next to the bathroom. The back of Penelope's head hit the wall, and her grip around his neck loosened. She dropped to the floor and began grabbing at his coat as she got to her knees. Penelope grabbed hold of his legs and held tight. Donald tried to pull away but stumbled. When Penelope couldn't hold on any longer, he turned and kicked her in the chest.

She couldn't breathe. He'd knocked the wind out of her with one kick, and she staggered on her hands and knees. The edges of her vision went gray and started to fuzz over like they had at Nate's store and again at the tennis courts.

Penelope gritted her teeth and closed her eyes. A small breath pushed through into her lungs, and she welcomed it, then focused on pulling in even more the next time.

A weak cry from Nadia caused her to open her eyes again. She pulled herself up to her knees and pulled in as much air as she could. She looked around the room, not seeing anything she could use as a weapon. Her eyes fell on the IV stand hooked up to Nadia's arm.

Standing up, Penelope made her way to the bed. His hands were at Nadia's throat again, and he squeezed slowly like he was enjoying watching her terror.

"This is over," Penelope said. She picked up the IV pole behind him and swung, crashing Donald on the side of the head.

He let go and fell to the floor. Penelope stood over him with the pole, ready to swing again if he got to his feet. A clear plastic tube had pulled from Nadia's arm, and saline solution dripped onto the floor.

"He's there," the nurse shouted from the doorway. Two officers rushed past her into the room.

"Put it down, ma'am," the nearest one said. He motioned with his hand for her to lower the IV pole.

Penelope kept her eyes on Don, who lay with his hand over his head, sobbing on the floor.

Chapter Forty-Nine

A week later, Penelope wiped the edges of two matching plates. She'd grilled two T-bone steaks to perfection with wood chips behind the lake house and made a roasted potato medley with fresh rosemary. A large wooden bowl of salad sat in the center of the kitchen table, the lettuce picked fresh that day from the Truegoods' vegetable garden.

"Penelope," Nate said from the back door of the kitchen.

"Come in," Penelope smiled, greeting him at the door. He clutched a bottle of wine in his hand and entered nervously.

"Smells great in here," Nate said, placing the bottle on the counter.

Penelope opened the oven and pulled out a loaf of homemade bread to cool on the countertop. "Thanks," she said. "I'm glad you could make it for dinner."

"I'd never pass up a dinner with you," Nate said. "Although I was picturing somewhere other than here." He looked uneasily around the old kitchen.

Penelope blushed and smiled. She opened the bottle of wine and poured two glasses, urging Nate to take a seat at the table. He hesitated, standing behind one of them.

"Nathaniel," Jeremiah said from the dining room doorway.

Nate's smile faded and was replaced by a lock of resignation. "Hi, Jerry."

Jeremiah smiled. "That's when I know I'm home. When someone calls me Jerry."

"You two have a seat," Penelope said, pulling out one of the chairs and motioning to Nate.

The two men seemed to square off with each other, neither wanting to be the first to move toward the table.

"The potatoes are getting cold," Penelope said to Nate. She flicked her eyes from his face to the chair.

Jeremiah made the first move and sat down. Nate gave Penelope a half smile and did the same. Penelope poured them each some wine. She turned back to the counter and used a knife to slice the bread, setting it in between the men with a ramekin of homemade herb butter.

"From your cows," Penelope said.

"Penelope convinced me," Jeremiah began, "that it was time we took another look at the arrangement we've made at the farm. And the other businesses around town."

Nate looked at him in disbelief. "I've been trying to talk to you for years. With zero success."

Jeremiah took one of his large hands and placed it gently on Nate's shoulder. "I should have listened. I'm sorry."

Penelope slipped out the back door of the kitchen and made her way back to the boat house, hiding a wide smile under her hand.

Chapter Fifty

"Are you staying here? Or coming with us when we leave?" Penelope asked.

Tama sat on one of the lounge chairs on the deck next to Penelope.

"I haven't decided yet," Tama said.

"That's understandable," Penelope said, nodding. "Of course, I'd love to keep you on. You're a bright talent, great to work with."

"I'm worried…what if the restaurant doesn't work? Will Jeremiah blame me?" Tama asked as she twisted her slender hands together in her lap.

"I've found Jeremiah is a man who can be reasoned with. Eventually," Penelope said. "That said, it's a big responsibility, launching a restaurant. Failure rate—"

"I know, I know. Ninety percent fail in the first year," Tama said, sighing. "I'm just so drawn to him. When I picture my future, I see Jeremiah in it."

"Then you should take a chance," Penelope said. "You know he's not always going to be here. He'll be off making movies all around the world."

"I've thought about that too," Tama said. "What would you do if you were me?"

Penelope looked into the young woman's eyes. Tama was a different kind of girl, young and beautiful, almost fragile-looking, but Penelope knew she had a steely spirit and a unique way of viewing the world.

"I can't tell you what I'd do," Penelope said. "Our lives are on different paths. Very different. The best advice I can give is to do what your heart and gut tell you to do, be smart about your choices, and push yourself out of your comfort zone. Wherever that zone lies for you."

Tama smiled. "You're not old enough to be this wise," she said.

Penelope laughed. "I've been on my own a long time. You pick things up along the way."

Chapter Fifty-One

Filming began the next day after the crew's week off. Jeremiah thought after Nadia's attack on the set that the overall energy was off. During their break, he offered daily yoga and meditation sessions and brought in a team of counselors for anyone who might need help processing what happened.

Breakfast was underway, and Penelope spotted Nevan, the on-set historian.

"How's your omelet?" Penelope asked. "I hope it's to your liking."

"It is, thanks," Nevan said, meeting her eyes. "Care to join me?"

Penelope reached into her apron pocket and pulled out the listening device she'd found in the boat house's living room. "I think you left something behind when you visited the last time."

Nevan took a sip of coffee and stared at the button on the white tablecloth.

"I'm not sure I follow," he said, gazing back up at her.

"I saw your name in a magazine. You contributed to the article about Heather Matthews in *THEM* about her death. I also found an article in her hometown paper written by you. My question is, why listen in on me?"

Nevan cleared his throat and set his coffee mug down. "Please, sit," he said quietly. Penelope reluctantly sat down in the chair opposite him and crossed her arms over her chest.

"I was helping the family," Nevan said. "So, I thought."

"By bugging my living quarters?" Penelope asked.

"I won't admit to that," Nevan said quickly. "You and Nadia, you're old friends. I assumed she'd be visiting you. My hope was she would confide something they could use for their civil suit," Nevan said. "I'm not proud of it, but Nadia shouldn't be either. Heather's family is devastated emotionally and bankrupt financially. Donald was at the end of his rope, and he saw Nadia as the source of his pain. I tried to tell him it wasn't worth it, that harming her wouldn't solve anything, but he didn't listen. Well, he did at first, but then…"

"I suppose you gathered Nadia never came to the boat house," Penelope said.

"True," Nevan said. "But she spent plenty of time in the main house."

"Did you bug her room, too?"

"I can't admit to that either. I have a respectable position I won't willingly jeopardize," Nevan said. "Heather was a wonderful girl, a rising star in the tennis world, but also impressionable. Nadia, who she looked to as a mentor, led her down a path she couldn't come back from, whether she meant to or not."

Penelope looked away from him and saw Tama standing by a table near the far end of the tent, talking with a few members of the crew. The sun lit her from the back, and she seemed to glow.

"I agree," Penelope said, looking back at him. "Mentors should lead, give good advice. But personal responsibility has to be at the forefront. You can't blame others for mistakes you make, or for not taking a path that opens to you. It's up to the individual."

"Tell that to the grieving family," Nevan countered.

"So, you admit you bugged my house?" Penelope said.

"I don't," Nevan said. "I might have dropped something when I retrieved the book. But nothing more than that."

Chapter Fifty-Two

"I'll be home in a few weeks," Penelope said to Joey over the phone the next day.

"I can't wait to see you."

"How is everyone there," Penelope said. "Have you talked to Lois?"

"Yes, the Letourneaus have been having a better time of it lately. We were able to make the case on the two robberies. These boys had the idea they'd start themselves a robbing crew to support their hockey club. They hit a few small businesses in town then hop the train, dodge the fares back to the city, just like you said."

"Jeez," Penelope said.

"I know," Joey said. "They didn't count on Sonya dying, so now they're in a lot more trouble than they anticipated when they started out."

"Why Sonya's and Lois's places?" Penelope asked.

"They figured they were easy targets, families with kids wouldn't fight back."

"Why was he saying *platit*? 'Pay' in Russian?" Penelope said.

"They fancied themselves gangsters, demanding to be paid."

"I can't believe that," Penelope said. "I hope they go away for a long time."

"Well, with Sonya's death and the assaults on half a dozen people, we have a good case. They're juvies though, so they won't be gone forever."

Penelope's stomach flipped, but she ignored it. "How's your partner?" Penelope asked.

"Looks like she'll be sticking around a while longer," Joey said. His normal irritation when he spoke about Clarissa was still there, but had lessened greatly. "She uncovered the thief in the property room. When you get home, you'll have to file a claim for your missing money to get reimbursed."

"Who was it?" Penelope asked.

"Night shift woman, only been here for a year. She ran into some money issues and started lifting things. Small at first. Clarissa got her in a sting, dropped off another designer bag in evidence, then followed it to see what happened."

"Oh my goodness," Penelope said. "That's amazing."

"Yeah, she sold it to a fence. We think Nadia's bag, too. That one she replaced with a knockoff from one of those street guys in Chinatown. But we think we'll be able to track it down for her."

"She'll be thrilled if you can," Penelope said.

"Yeah," Joey said. "So Clarissa has been offered a permanent spot here. She's still thinking about her next move. I might have my first permanent partner. We'll see."

"I think you make a good team," Penelope said.

"She knows how to push my buttons," Joey said. "But she's good police."

Penelope peered out the windshield at the boarded-up service station. Tama paced in front of it slowly, looking at the ground in front of her, then paused to look back at the building.

"Has everything quieted down in Vermont?" Joey asked.

Penelope sighed. "Yes, Donald Matthews is under arrest for criminal assault. Nadia had her first surgery on her arm last week. The doctors are optimistic, but it remains to be seen if she'll ever play tennis again.

At least professionally."

"That's got to be a blow," Joey said. "Maybe she could coach, if it comes to that."

Penelope thought about the herbal supplements, the competition, and Heather Matthews. "I'm not sure what path she'll take. But I'm glad she survived, both getting run off the road and what happened at the house."

Tama stood at the front door of the service station and ran her finger between two plywood boards.

"I'm glad you survived, too," Joey said. "I've been making a list, saving some properties we might want to look at when you get home."

Penelope smiled, picturing her and Joey looking for a home together, wondering what it might look like.

"Can't wait," she said.

Organic Butternut Squash Soup

Ingredients:

- Organic butternut squash, peeled and diced
- Apples, peeled and chopped
- Vegetable broth
- Onion, garlic, and ginger (for flavor)
- Vermont maple syrup
- Salt, pepper, and nutmeg to taste
- Olive oil for roasting

Instructions:

1. Roast butternut squash, apples, onion, garlic, and ginger with olive oil until tender.
2. Blend the roasted ingredients with vegetable broth until smooth.
3. Transfer the mixture to a pot, add maple syrup, salt, pepper, and nutmeg.
4. Simmer for a few minutes, adjusting seasoning to taste.

Vermont Harvest Salad

Ingredients:

- Mixed greens
- Heirloom tomatoes, sliced
- Roasted beets, sliced
- Local goat cheese, crumbled
- Maple-balsamic vinaigrette (maple syrup, balsamic vinegar, olive oil, Dijon mustard, salt, and pepper)

Instructions:

1. Toss mixed greens with sliced tomatoes, roasted beets, and crumbled goat cheese.
2. Whisk together the vinaigrette ingredients and drizzle over the salad.

Clam Bake

Ingredients:

- 1 dozen clams, scrubbed
- 1 pound mussels, cleaned and debearded
- 1 pound local sausage, sliced
- 4 ears of corn, shucked and halved
- 1 pound baby potatoes, halved
- 1 onion, sliced
- 4 cloves garlic, minced
- 1/2 cup white wine
- 2 tablespoons fresh parsley, chopped
- Salt and pepper to taste

Instructions:

1. Preheat the oven to 425°F (220°C).
2. In a large roasting pan or on a baking sheet, arrange the clams, mussels, sausage, corn, potatoes, onion, and garlic.
3. Pour the white wine over the ingredients and season with salt and pepper.
4. Cover the pan tightly with foil and bake in the preheated oven for about 25-30 minutes or until the clams and mussels have opened.
5. Carefully remove from the oven, discard any unopened clams or mussels.

6. Sprinkle with fresh parsley and serve directly from the pan. Enjoy your New England-inspired clam bake!

Pumpkin and Cranberry Quinoa Pilaf

Ingredients:

- 1 cup quinoa, rinsed
- 2 cups roasted pumpkin or butternut squash, diced
- 1/2 cup dried cranberries
- 1/4 cup toasted pumpkin seeds
- 1/2 teaspoon ground cinnamon
- 1/4 teaspoon ground nutmeg
- Salt and pepper to taste
- 2 tablespoons maple syrup

Instructions:

1. Cook the quinoa according to package instructions.
2. In a large bowl, combine the cooked quinoa, roasted pumpkin or squash, dried cranberries, and toasted pumpkin seeds.
3. In a small bowl, mix together the cinnamon, nutmeg, salt, pepper, and maple syrup.
4. Drizzle the spice mixture over the quinoa mixture and toss gently to combine.
5. Adjust seasoning to taste and serve warm.

Stuffed Acorn Squash

Ingredients:

- Acorn squash, halved and seeds removed
- Quinoa, cooked
- Mixed vegetables (e.g., bell peppers, zucchini, mushrooms), chopped
- Sage-infused brown butter (butter, fresh sage)
- Sautéed kale or Swiss chard

Instructions:

1. Roast acorn squash until tender.
2. Mix cooked quinoa with sautéed vegetables.
3. Stuff the acorn squash halves with the quinoa and vegetable mixture.
4. Drizzle with sage-infused brown butter.
5. Serve with sautéed kale or Swiss chard on the side.

Roasted Root Vegetables

Ingredients:

- Assorted root vegetables (carrots, parsnips, sweet potatoes, etc.)
- Olive oil, garlic, rosemary, salt, and pepper

Instructions:

1. Wash and chop the root vegetables into uniform pieces.
2. Toss with olive oil, minced garlic, rosemary, salt, and pepper.
3. Roast until vegetables are caramelized and tender.

Blueberry Oat Muffins

Ingredients:

- 1 cup whole wheat flour
- 1 cup oats
- 1 teaspoon baking powder
- 1/2 teaspoon baking soda
- 1/4 teaspoon salt
- 1/2 cup yogurt
- 1/4 cup melted coconut oil or olive oil
- 1/4 cup maple syrup or local honey
- 1 teaspoon vanilla extract
- 1 cup fresh blueberries

Instructions:

1. Preheat the oven to 350°F (175°C) and line a muffin tin with paper liners.
2. In a large bowl, combine the whole wheat flour, oats, baking powder, baking soda, and salt.
3. In another bowl, whisk together the yogurt, melted coconut oil or olive oil, maple syrup or honey, and vanilla extract.
4. Pour the wet ingredients into the dry ingredients and stir until just combined.
5. Gently fold in the fresh blueberries.

6. Spoon the batter into the muffin cups, filling each about 2/3 full.

7. Bake for 18-20 minutes or until a toothpick inserted into the center comes out clean.

8. Allow the muffins to cool for a few minutes in the tin before transferring them to a wire rack to cool completely.

Cocktail Ideas for a Sustainable Life

Gin and Tonic:

Ingredients: Locally distilled gin, tonic water, organic cucumber slices, and fresh mint.

Serve in reusable glassware, and consider using a stainless steel or bamboo straw.

Farm-to-Glass Mojito:

Ingredients: Organic white rum, fresh lime juice, organic mint leaves, and locally sourced simple syrup.

Use a bamboo muddler and serve over crushed ice in a reusable glass.

Seasonal Berry Basil Smash:

Ingredients: Muddled seasonal berries (blueberries, raspberries), organic vodka, fresh basil leaves, and a splash of organic elderflower liqueur.

Garnish with a basil sprig and serve in a glass made from recycled materials.

Locavore Lemonade:

Ingredients: Locally produced vodka, freshly squeezed lemon juice, organic agave syrup, and a splash of sparkling water.

Serve in a glass with a lemon wheel and reusable straw.

Eco-Friendly Espresso Martini:

Ingredients: Organic vodka or coffee liqueur, cold brew coffee made from fair-trade beans, and a touch of organic agave syrup.

Shake with ice and strain into a chilled glass, garnish with locally sourced coffee beans.

Herb-Infused Tequila Sunrise:

Ingredients: Organic tequila, fresh-squeezed orange juice, a splash of pomegranate juice, and a sprig of rosemary or thyme.

Serve over ice and garnish with an orange twist.

Cucumber Basil Gimlet:

Ingredients: Locally distilled gin or vodka, fresh lime juice, organic cucumber slices, and basil leaves.

Shake with ice, strain, and serve in a chilled glass. Garnish with a cucumber wheel and basil leaf.

Maple Bourbon Old Fashioned:

Ingredients: Locally distilled bourbon, organic maple syrup, a dash of bitters, and an orange twist.

Serve over a large ice cube in a reusable whiskey glass.

Remember to choose organic and locally sourced spirits, use fresh, seasonal produce, and opt for reusable bar tools and glassware. Additionally, consider implementing sustainable practices, such as using a compost bin for fruit scraps and promoting responsible consumption.

A Note from the Author

This second edition of a book I wrote over a decade ago has been revised and re-edited, updated in places, and hopefully improved upon. If it's your second time around, I appreciate the continued support. If you're meeting Penelope and the gang for the first time, welcome! It's been quite a journey since I first sat down and created this world and these characters. It's felt like a homecoming, with all of the related emotions those inspire, breathing new life into the series. I'm grateful to my fans and readers for their warm encouragement.

The recipes are a new addition to the books. During my college years, I spent a lot of time in Vermont and became curious about the unique ways of life there. I met so many people who were really concerned with the environment, sustainability, and food waste. Visiting the green rolling hills and wide-open spaces was such a stark contrast with New York City, which could seem so dirty and wasteful in comparison. I read an article about movies being at the top of the most environmentally impactful industries at the time I wrote this book, and that influenced the theme and recipes I've included. I always strive to source food as close as I can to my home, with the least amount of processing possible, and I think if we all did that, our planet would thank us in return. I hope you enjoy and are inspired to create culinary magic of your own as a result.

Acknowledgements

This book is about family, the one you're born with and the one you create as you go. I'd like to thank everyone in mine, near and far, here and gone, with all my heart.

About the Author

Shawn Reilly Simmons is a novelist and two-time Agatha Award-winning short story writer based in Frederick, Maryland. Cooking behind the scenes on movie sets perfectly combined two of her great passions: movies, and food, and provides the inspiration for the Red Carpet Catering mystery series.

SOCIAL MEDIA HANDLES:
    https://www.facebook.com/ShawnReillySimmonsAuthor
    https://twitter.com/ShawnRSimmons
    https://www.instagram.com/shawnrsimmons/

AUTHOR WEBSITE:
    https://www.shawnreillysimmons.com/

Also by Shawn Reilly Simmons

<u>Novels</u>

The Red Carpet Catering Mysteries
  Murder On A Silver Platter
  Murder On The Half Shell
  Murder On A Designer Diet
  Murder Is The Main Course
  Murder On The Rocks
  Murder With All The Trimmings
  Murder On The Chopping Block

Upcoming Titles!
  Murder On The Side
  Murder À La Carte

<u>Short Stories</u>

2016

  "A Gathering of Great Detectives" - published in *Malice Domestic 11: Mystery Most Conventional*
  "Look Away" – published in Windward: The Best New England Crime Stories

2017

  "The Prodigy" - published in *Mystery Tour:* Crime Writers' Association Anthology
  "Burnt Orange" - published in *Passport To Murder*: The 2017 Bouchercon Anthology

"Play Dead" – published in *Busted*: Arresting Stories from the Beat

"Farm to Table" – published in *Snowbound:* The Best New England Crime Stories

"You Always Hurt the One You Love" – published in *Malice Domestic 12: Mystery Most Historical*

"Humble Pie" – published In *Noir At The Salad Bar:* Culinary Tales With A Bite

2018

"Death on the Beach" – published in *Malice Domestic 13: Mystery Most Geographical*

"Downcity Detective" - published in *Landfall:* The Best New England Crime Stories

2019

"The Last Word" – published In *Malice Domestic 14: Mystery Most Edible**

"Sweet Tawny Breeze" - published in *After Midnight*: The Writers' Police Academy Anthology

"Stolen Moments" – published in *Seascape*: The Best New England Crime Stories

2020

"Now is the Hour" - published in *Writers Crushing Covid-19*

"Dance on Fire" - published in *Malice Domestic 15: Mystery Most Theatrical*

*"The Red Herrings at Killington Inn" - published in *Masthead:* The Best New England Crime Stories

2021

*"Bay of Reckoning" - published in *Murder On The Beach:* A

Destination Murders Short Story Collection

"From Whiskey to Wine" - published in *Murder By The Glass*

2022

"A Perfect Climb" - published in *Murder In The Mountains: A Destinations Murder Short Story Collection*

"A Death in Four Parts" - published in *Music Of The Night: The Crime Writers' Association Anthology*

"The Devil's in the Details" - published in *Malice Domestic 17: Mystery Most Diabolical*

2023

"Two if By Sea" – published in *Murder At Sea*

"Killer Cupcakes" – published in *Malice Domestic 18: Mystery Most Traditional*

*Nominated for the Agatha Award for Best Short Story

**Winner of the Agatha Award for Best Short Story

**Anthony Award Finalist for Best Anthology or Collection

www.ingramcontent.com/pod-product-compliance
Lightning Source LLC
Chambersburg PA
CBHW050158120726

47903CB00002B/666